S0-AGG-120

BEACON STREET GIRLS

This book belongs to:

VERITAS AMICITIA GAUDIUM
truth friendship fun

TM

"My name is Charlotte Ramsey. I've traveled all over the world with my dad. Now I'm flying back to Paris to find my lost cat!"

BEACON STREET GIRLS

Be sure to read all of our books:

Copyright © 2006 by B*tween Productions, Inc.,
Home of the Beacon Street Girls.
Beacon Street Girls, Kgirl, B*tween Productions, B*Street, and the
characters Maeve, Avery, Charlotte, Isabel, Katani, Marty, Nick,
Anna, Joline, and Happy Lucky Thingy
are registered trademarks and/or copyrights of B*tween Productions, Inc.

All rights reserved. No part of this book may be reproduced in any form or by
any electronic or mechanical means, including information storage and retrieval
systems, without permission in writing from the publisher, except by a reviewer
who may quote brief passages in a review. If you purchased this book without a
cover, you should be aware that this book is stolen property. It was reported as
"unsold and destroyed" to the publisher, and neither the author nor the
publisher has received any payment for this "stripped book."

First Edition

The characters and events in this book are fictitious.
Any similarity to real persons, living or dead, is coincidental and not
intended by the author. References to real people, events, establishments,
artwork, organizations, products, or locales are
intended only to provide a sense of authenticity,
and are not to be construed as endorsements.

Series Editor: Roberta MacPhee
Art Direction: Pamela M. Esty
Book Design: Dina Barsky
Illustration: Pamela M. Esty
Cover photograph: Digital composition
Special thanks to Emma Balmuth-Loris for photos from Paris.

Produced by B*tween Productions, Inc.
1666 Massachusetts Avenue, Suite 17
Lexington, MA 02420

ISBN: 1-933566-00-0

CIP data is available at the Library of Congress
10 9 8 7 6 5 4 3 2 1

Printed in Canada

Visit the Beacon Street Girls at beaconstreetgirls.com

BEACON STREET GIRLS

Charlotte in Paris

La Meilleure Nouvelle

THE BEST NEWS EVER

To: Charlotte
From: Sophie
Subject: Orangina

i have seen Orangina!
it was him
i'm so sure ... he was wandering by the
Seine
i call his name and he turn around
i took only 1 step in his direction and
he ran away
you must come. he would come to you if
you called him
i worry about him ... alone with no
charming houseboat to return to at
night
i have a few days off from school

because of teacher meetings next week
i'll talk to *maman*. you talk to your
father
you must come to Paris!
Orangina needs you
And you have been away much too long!

bisous﹁
Sophie

IT TOOK ME HOURS to fall asleep that night. Too many visions of a sugar plum Orangina were dancing in my head. The next morning, I jumped out of bed as soon as my alarm went off, and I rushed to the kitchen to tell Dad about the email. When I got to the part about Sophie begging me to come to Paris, I began to talk faster and faster. It was like I was on *fast forward*.

"I know—it's short notice, but Dad, it's such good timing. I don't have any tests next week, and I miss Sophie so much! It feels like forever since I've seen her! Can you believe she found Orangina? I looked online last night at flights, and they're actually really cheap right now, and we don't have school next Friday because it's a professional day, *and* I haven't missed a day of school yet this year *and* ..." I had to stop and take a deep breath. I was trying to stay calm, but it wasn't easy.

"So?" I asked tentatively. My dad is pretty laid back as far as dads go, but still ... I knew it was a real long shot.

I mean, who sends their daughter to Paris to find a missing cat?

"Are you *really* asking me if you can jet off to Paris next week ... alone?" Dad looked amused.

"Well ... uhh ... uhh ... actually ... yes." I crossed my fingers behind my back and tapped my foot on the floor. It's what I do when I want something really, really badly.

Dad stirred his cinnamon oatmeal around and around and looked thoughtful. "I don't know, Charlotte. I'd love to be able to just say yes and send you off on a great adventure. I know Orangina means a lot to you, and how much you miss Sophie. But there are a lot of things to think about. It's a big deal to miss a week of school." My dad teaches creative writing at Boston University, so school is very important to him. He continued, "I know *I* hate to see my students miss a class ... it's hard to catch up. Even if tickets are cheap, it's still a significant amount of money. And to be honest, I don't know how I feel about sending you off on a plane all by yourself. We've always traveled together."

I took a deep breath and launched into the responses I had rehearsed before falling asleep the night before. "I can talk to my teachers before I leave, and I know the BSG will collect all of my assignments. I'm doing really well in school, and I'll work extra hard before I leave and even harder when I get back. Besides, I still have some money saved from my birthday last year that I could put toward the ticket. And I know I've never traveled by myself before, but plenty of kids my age do it. Avery's flown by

❧

herself to see her dad in Colorado a couple of times. And I'm sure the Morels would meet me as soon as I got off the plane. Besides," I paused to catch my breath, "Traveling is *very* educational."

Dad laughed out loud. I knew that last comment would crack him up. It's something he was *always* telling me.

"Well, Charlotte, you've presented a good case for yourself, that's for sure. Maybe you should think about becoming a lawyer. Did you memorize your speech, or was that a spur of the moment thing?" he asked with a smile.

"A little bit of both," I admitted.

"Charlotte, I know how much a trip back to Paris would mean to you, but I need to think about this. This is not trivial. We can talk about it later tonight."

"OK," I agreed. Suddenly, I felt a little bit optimistic. At least it wasn't an outright "NO."

Just as I was pouring myself a glass of orange juice, the phone rang. Dad picked it up, and I froze in my tracks. "Oh, *bonjour*, Jacqueline." It was Madame Morel—Sophie's mom. Dad motioned me out of the room. I sighed and took my orange juice and oatmeal into the hallway, but I lurked at the door. I just *had* to hear what my dad was saying.

Marty trotted down the hallway and sat on my foot, begging for oatmeal. I peered around the doorway and tried to get a sense of how the conversation was going. Dad mostly listened. I chuckled to myself. Madame Morel was a real talker. Marty's little doggie ears perked up every time Dad said anything, but Marty never took his eyes off

"When I first moved to Brookline, Maeve,
Katani, Avery, Isabel, and I formed a club called
the Beacon Street Girls."

~ pg. 7

the oatmeal. The little dude loves his snacks.

"*Oui*, yes, I know … I agree … I hope so too … thanks for calling, it was nice to hear your voice again … I'm sure you understand what's going on here … Talk to you soon, Jacqueline. *Au revoir*." My father hung up the phone.

"Charlotte!"

I waited a few seconds before walking back into the kitchen, even though I knew that Dad knew I had been listening. "Yes?"

"You need to give me time to think this whole thing over. As I said, I'm not making a decision right now. Not even a phone call from Paris will change that. OK?"

"OK."

"And try not to get your hopes up either."

"I'll try."

That would be easier said than done. It was hard not to hope. Madame Morel could be a very convincing woman. I had a feeling that whatever she had just said may have tipped the scales in my favor!

When I arrived that morning at Ms. Rodriguez' homeroom, Maeve was sitting on the edge of her desk, chatting a mile a minute with Katani and Isabel.

"Char!" Maeve exclaimed as I dropped my bag on my desk. "There's a substitute in for Mr. Sherman today. Isn't that great?" Mr. Sherman, the math teacher nicknamed "the Crow," was Maeve's least favorite teacher.

Maeve could make anyone excited about anything. She was dramatic and bubbly, and just an all around fun person to be around. Most importantly, she was one of my best friends. When I first moved to Brookline, Maeve, Katani, Avery, and I formed a club called the Beacon Street Girls. Then Isabel moved to Brookline a few weeks into the school year, and now the five of us are best friends.

Before I had a chance to answer Maeve, Avery came barreling through the door. She dropped her duffle bag and quickly gathered her hair up in her favorite soccer ball hair tie. "I thought I was going to be late! I couldn't find my math book—somehow it ended up next to Walter's tank in my closet." Avery's pet snake, Walter, was actually kind of cute. A total pet lover, it's her dream to get a dog of her own someday, but her mom's allergy to furry pets makes that impossible. That's why Marty has lived with me ever since we found him in a garbage can. The BSG all love Marty, but Avery has a real soft spot for him.

Maeve shuddered. "Eeeew … I don't know which is worse … math or snakes." Maeve's learning problems sometimes made school hard for her. Nothing could stop that girl's talent on stage, though. She was headed straight for Hollywood!

"Snakes. Definitely snakes." Katani shuddered as she smoothed her newly cut bangs over her forehead. She was looking stylish as usual that morning, wearing a knee-length skirt that she had designed and sewn herself.

I couldn't hold it in any longer. "I … I might be going

to Paris," I blurted out.

"What?!" Maeve exclaimed.

"Are you serious, Char?" Isabel asked.

"I'm completely serious. But I'm not sure if it'll actually happen yet." I filled the BSG in on the whole story, starting with the email from Sophie and ending with Dad's warning not to get my hopes up.

"Parents always say that. I bet he'll let you go. He would've said no already if he was against it," Avery speculated.

"I hope you're right, Ave … but sometimes when my mom says don't get your hopes up, she still ends up saying no. It's the worst," Katani concluded.

"My Aunt Lourdes does that too. But I think it'll be impossible for you *not* to get your hopes up, Char. So let's just talk about Paris … you'll be thinking about it all day anyway." Isabel's eyes sparkled as she listed the Paris museums and art galleries she wanted to visit someday. "Oh, and the Musée d'Orsay! I think that would be my absolute favorite. Cézanne's *Apples and Oranges*, Van Gogh's *The Siesta* … Did you guys know that the museum was built in an old train station?"

As the bell rang and the last stragglers raced into homeroom, I listened to my friends' excited chatter about Paris and wondered what the day would bring. Isabel was right … it was impossible *not* to get my hopes up. I crossed my fingers … for Orangina, for Sophie, for Paris, and for a new adventure.

I usually paid close attention in school and always took detailed notes, but by last period social studies class on Wednesday afternoon, I couldn't control my nervous energy. I tried to sit still, but it was hopeless … my foot began tapping spontaneously. It just wouldn't stop. Travel was in my bones and Sophie's invitation to visit Paris had gotten me so excited that sitting still was not an option. As soon as the bell rang, I raced out the door, quickly catching up to Avery.

"Hey Char, basketball practice was cancelled today … want to take Marty for a run with me?" asked Avery, jogging backward toward the seventh-grade lockers.

"That sounds good, Ave … I won't be able to start my homework right now anyway … I'm too nervous about this whole Paris thing."

"Want me to see if I can convince your dad? My mom tells me I'm very persistent," Avery offered with a grin.

"That's probably not a good idea, Ave. You know how my dad doesn't react very well to nagging, and he already got a phone call from Madame Morel encouraging him to say yes." I hoped Avery wouldn't get some crazy scheme into her head to try and help … that could be disastrous.

"Hey, Charlotte!" Chelsea Briggs called out, hurrying down the hall toward Avery and me.

"Hi Chelsea," I said. "What's going on?"

"Maeve told me you're going to Paris!" she said. "That's awesome."

✣

"*Might* be going to Paris," I corrected her. "My dad hasn't given me permission yet. It's still up in the air." I suddenly wished I hadn't said anything about the trip. Soon the rumor would be all over school, and I'd feel really silly if it was all for nothing.

"Well, if you do end up going, you can borrow my digital camera," Chelsea offered. "Maybe you could take a few pics for *The Sentinel*." As the newspaper's official photographer, Chelsea was always looking for exciting photo opportunities.

"Thanks, Chels. That's really nice of you. My digital broke a few weeks ago."

"No prob. Just let me know, and I can drop it off at your house. See you guys later." Chelsea waved good-bye and jogged off in the other direction.

When Avery and I reached the seventh-grade lockers, I quickly loaded up my bag and grabbed my jacket.

"Race you!" Avery shouted as soon as we got to the outside doors. Usually when she said that, I didn't take her up on the challenge, but that day I felt like a run might actually calm me down. I made it to the doorstep of our yellow Victorian house only about 10 seconds behind Avery.

"Wow, Char ... you're totally on fire today!" Avery was impressed.

I caught my breath as I unlocked the door and held it open for Avery. We both ran up the stairs to the upper part of the house where Dad and I live.

"Ruffff! Wooof, wooooof!" Marty barked happily

when he heard our voices.

"Hey buddy, did ya miss me?" Avery sat on the floor in the hallway and Marty hopped into her lap.

"Hi girls." My dad walked out of the kitchen to greet Avery and me.

"Hi Mr. Ramsey," Avery replied with a huge smile.

"Hey Dad." I searched his face for clues, wondering if he had made his decision yet. *Nothing*. "We're going to take Marty for a W-A-L-K." (We have to spell out the word "walk" so Marty doesn't go nuts.)

"Good idea. The little guy's got even more energy than usual today. Charlotte, can I talk to you in the kitchen for a minute before you go?"

I looked back at Avery as I followed my dad through the hallway. She was holding Marty's front paws up … crossed for good luck.

Dad sat down at the kitchen table and motioned for me to do the same.

"Here's the deal, Charlotte. I spent the entire day thinking about Paris. I made a list of the pros and cons. I even asked the opinions of a couple of other professors that have kids your age. I finally decided that one pro outweighed all the cons … you've moved around much more than most kids your age, and I know it hasn't always been easy. You've had to leave friends behind, and you've always been a good sport about it. So … I want you to go on this trip and have the time of your life. But … there's one condition. It will be the most cautious, responsible,

CAREFUL time of your life, understand?"

"Really? I can go?! I can go?! Wooooohoooo!" I whooped, jumping up to hug Dad. "Thank you, Dad! You're the best! A trip to Paris ... this is unbelievable!"

"Wooooohooooo!" Avery echoed from the hallway and raced in to give me a high five.

"Woooof!" barked Marty in agreement.

PARTY TIME

Late Saturday morning, Dad and I were doing the dishes from our yummy blueberry pancake breakfast when the phone rang.

"Hello? Yes, she is. Hold on just a second. ... It's Maeve," he motioned, handing the phone to me.

"It's all set," she chirped. "A going-away party for you at Montoya's at 4 o'clock ... BSG style fabulous!" Maeve, the self-pronounced social director of the Beacon Street Girls, announced breathlessly.

I covered the receiver and told Dad what Maeve had said. He raised an eyebrow doubtfully ... I knew exactly what he was thinking. He wasn't crazy about the idea of a last-minute party. Ever since he gave me permission to go to Paris, Dad had been a nervous wreck, running around and making phone calls back and forth with the airlines and the Morels as he chaotically tried to help me get ready.

"But I still have to buy a present for the Morels. I bet they'd like something from a local place ... like one of Montoya's gift baskets," I suggested to Dad before he could veto the party. "I promise I'll only stay for an hour … just long enough to say good-bye to the BSG and buy the gift. Please, Dad? Please … ?"

Dad nodded reluctantly. "All right. I have to run some errands, so I'll drop you off and pick you up. Make sure you get all of your packing finished before you go … we're leaving for the airport at 5 o'clock sharp."

I raced upstairs to my room to put all the clothes I'd laid out into my suitcase and double-check my list. I still couldn't believe it was happening. It was a dream come true … my very own adventure back to Paris!

From all my traveling with Dad, I've learned that the best way to pack is to make a list and check off each thing as you put it in the suitcase … that way you don't end up with sneakers and no socks, or socks and no sneakers, or one T-shirt and four pairs of jeans.

Just as I was about to zip up my suitcase, Marty hopped inside and poked his head over the rim.

"Sorry, little dude, I wish you could come to Paris, but you have to stay here and keep Dad company, OK? And that's a really important job, just so you know."

"Ruuuuuffff!" Marty leapt onto the floor and pitter-pattered to the kitchen, where I could hear Dad talking to him. I think people talk to their dogs because dogs really seem to understand what they're saying … sometimes even better than other humans.

★

✤

Dad dropped me off in front of Montoya's Bakery at precisely 4 o'clock. "I'll be back in an hour to pick you up," he reminded me.

I waved as Dad pulled away from the curb. When I looked over my shoulder, I could see all four of them — Maeve, Avery, Katani, and Isabel — through the bakery window, waiting for me at a table. Avery waved.

I jogged to the door and pulled it open. The air was filled with the sweet aroma of freshly made cookies, hot chocolate, and cinnamon. *Mmmm*! I stopped at the counter first to order the gift basket for the Morels so I wouldn't forget.

"Are you all packed and ready?" Maeve asked when I made it to the table.

"I'm ready," I declared with a smile.

"*Paris*. I've always wanted to go to Paris," Maeve sighed. "The City of Light. The City of Love! So many of the great romantic movies were set there. It's where Audrey Hepburn and Cary Grant felt the magic spell of love in *Charade*. And, oh, who could ever forget *An American in Paris*? It was so dreamy."

Avery made a face. "What are you talking about, Maeve? You act like Charlotte is going to Paris for romance. She's going there to find Orangina and visit Sophie. Hey, Char, make sure you tell Miss Pierce I'll come over every day and take Marty for a run."

"OK, but I think she's excited about playing with him, too," I replied.

Even though Marty lived with me, he really belonged to all of us—after all, he was the official BSG mascot. We found the "little dude" abandoned in the park during the first week of school. We didn't know if we'd be able to keep him because Miss Pierce, my landlady, used to have a NO PETS rule. But it all worked out, and now Miss Pierce loved Marty like the rest of us. How could she not? He was irresistibly adorable! When she heard I was going to Paris, Miss Pierce said she would be glad to watch after the little guy whenever Dad's not around.

"You'll have time to do some shopping, won't you, Charlotte?" Katani asked.

"Shopping?" I was confused.

Katani was clearly horrified by my reaction. "Listen to me, Miss Charlotte Ramsey. Paris is one of the world's major fashion hotspots! I mean, as you're looking for Orangina, maybe you could check out the store windows on the Champs-Elysées for just a minute?" Of course, Katani, the fashion diva of our group, knew about the famous fashion streets of Paris. By what she was wearing—a rose-colored shirt with a drape neck, jeans, and tall black boots—it looked like she'd gone to Paris to pick out her outfit that very morning.

"Katani has a point. I mean, I know you're going to look for Orangina, but you'll have time to visit the museums, won't you?" Isabel asked. "Have you ever been to the Picasso Museum?"

"No," I admitted, a little embarrassed that I had lived

in Paris for so long and never visited one of its most famous museums. "But I did see some of Picasso's work at the Louvre. Maybe I'll have time to visit a museum or two, but I'm mostly excited to get Orangina back and see Sophie again."

"Picasso has lots of art in the Louvre, but the Picasso Museum has even more," Isabel said. "He spent a lot of time in Paris studying the works of other famous artists and working on his own pieces. His work is still influencing artists today." Isabel was usually pretty quiet, but she always lit up when she talked about something she loved. And art was definitely that something. I had a feeling that someday we'd see one of her paintings hanging in a museum. It would be so wonderful to walk around with my family and say, "Yes, that famous, world-renowned artist Isabel Martinez is one of my best friends."

"So you're really going to Paris?" Nick asked as he brought a tray of hot chocolate and muffins to the table. Nick Montoya was in our seventh-grade class. His parents owned Montoya's and Nick helped out. I really liked Nick, and he was always nice to me and the BSG. He was the only guy I knew who was really interested in all the places I had been in the world. Nick would be a great world traveler someday. Maybe he and I could hike the Himalayas together when we grew up!

I nodded. "Only for a week. I'm leaving tonight and I'll be back next Saturday afternoon. I'm going to visit Sophie and look for Orangina. Sophie said she saw him near our old houseboat. If I find Orangina, I'm going to bring him back home with me." I knew Nick would understand how important this trip was ... I'd told him all about Sophie and Orangina before.

"Do you think Marty likes cats?" Avery wondered.

"Even if he doesn't, he'll love Orangina," I assured her. Although secretly I wasn't quite certain that Marty could love any cat, even one as cool as Orangina.

"Time for presents!" Maeve announced as soon as Nick left the table.

"Presents? Are you serious? You didn't have to do that!" I exclaimed.

"What would a *bon voyage* party be without *bon voyage* presents?" Maeve reasoned.

"We couldn't let you leave without something to remember us by," Isabel said.

"But I'll only be gone a week," I protested.

"Me first!" Maeve insisted, pushing a small pink bag overflowing with hot pink tissue paper toward me.

I reached in. It was a pen on a cord, decorated Maeve-style with tiny gold and silver stars. Maeve knew how much I loved stargazing.

"This is so cool!" I exclaimed.

"Writers should never go anywhere without a pen! You know, you are going to write on your barf bag, but you need something to write *with*," Maeve said. "Besides, you might be inspired to start your first novel while walking along the Seine. You never know!"

"Thanks, Maeve," I said. "That was really thoughtful of you. Maybe when I publish my first novel, *Barf Bag Memories*, I'll dedicate it to you."

Maeve grimaced. Barf bags weren't exactly to her liking, but I liked to write a note on them every time I traveled on a plane.

"Me next," Avery said impatiently, pushing a crumpled brown paper bag in my direction. "Sorry, I didn't have time to wrap it." The presentation was so Avery.

I took a small notebook out of the bag.

"It'll fit in your back pocket. I didn't think you'd want to lug your journal through the streets of Paris. If you turn to the back pages, there's a little map of Paris there that I got off the Internet. I don't agree with Maeve ... I think you'll need a pen AND something to write on."

"Thanks, Avery. I'm going to try to fill the whole thing up in one week."

Katani pushed a lemon-colored bag forward. The top of the bag had been double-folded. Katani had punched two large holes in the double-fold, threaded a gauzy orange ribbon through the holes, tied the bag closed with a perfect bow, and included a card to match. I untied the ribbon, opened the bag, and found a knitted hat in a rich, royal purple ... my favorite color.

"Oh, Katani. It's beautiful ... and very stylish!" I exclaimed, pressing it to my cheek. It was the softest yarn I'd ever felt.

"Isn't it the coolest shade of purple? The bright color

will make your eyes pop and seem even more green than usual," she remarked.

"Did you make it?"

Katani nodded. "I'd already started it for you before I was sure about the Paris trip, but I worked faster these past couple of days and got it done just in time."

"Wow—it's wonderful. Thank you so much, Katani!" I remembered back to how Katani and I first met, and how she didn't want to be my friend. And now we were such good friends. Life was just so surprising sometimes.

"Last but not least ..." Isabel said, holding up the gift bag on her lap. She peeked inside. "It seems kind of silly now, but I thought it was perfect when I found it at the Book Nook. I really wanted to get you the book *The Ultimate Picasso*, but it was way too expensive. So I got you this instead. I hope you like it!"

"A Picasso coloring book?" Avery asked when I pulled the book from the bag. "Isabel, coloring books are for babies, not 12 year olds," she blurted out in her typical abrupt manner.

Isabel blushed. "It *is* a coloring book, but it's for kids our age, Avery. I thought Charlotte would want something to do on the plane. There's a set of colored pencils in there. It has all sorts of cool facts about Picasso too."

"I love it, Isabel. Thanks so much. I was looking for something to do on the plane, and this will be perfect." I was not a great artist, but I still liked to color. It could be super relaxing.

We barely had time to finish our hot chocolate and one of Montoya's famous muffins before Avery announced that she had seen my dad drive by the window.

"I better go ... my dad wants to head to the airport early in case there's traffic."

I gave them each a hug and they stacked the *bon voyage* gifts in my arms.

"Email us!" Maeve called as I hurried out the door.

I turned back to wave at the girls and nearly crashed into a man walking down the sidewalk.

"Wait! Wait!" Katani called as she rushed out the door toward me. "I forgot to ask you something."

"Sure, what is it?"

"OK, it's a big favor. I was wondering ... if it's not too much trouble," Katani started to say, suddenly seeming shy for a change. She thrust a small box into one of the gift bags in my arms. "It's a disposable camera. Would you take a few pictures of the clothes in Paris? I'm looking for some European inspiration for my Kgirl designs."

I promised Katani that I would take as many pictures as I could. Then the man in the car behind Dad blew his horn impatiently for the second time, so I hopped into our car and waved out the window as we drove down Harvard Street. Just as Dad was turning the corner onto Beacon, I suddenly remembered something. "Oops! Dad, can you pull over?"

"What's the matter? Are you OK?" he asked as he pulled into a parking spot, looking concerned.

"Yeah … I just forgot the Morels' gift basket." I jumped out onto the sidewalk and jogged back toward Montoya's Bakery.

Nick must have seen me coming, because he was waiting at the door of the bakery with the gift basket in his hands.

"Have a great trip, Charlotte. I want to hear all about Paris when you get back … especially the bakeries. Paris is supposed to be famous for its pastries, but are they any match for Montoya's?" Nick asked with grin.

"No, no of course not!" I laughed, taking the basket from him. "Thanks, Nick. There is no way I'm leaving Paris without at least one incredible story. I hope!"

II

Bon Voyage!
HAVE A GOOD TRIP!

BOSTON'S LOGAN AIRPORT was bustling when we got there. Dad was so nervous about me going on a plane by myself that he looked like he was going to have a heart attack. He was double-checking everything and asking me a billion questions.

"Do you have your boarding pass out? And your passport? You don't have to show your passport again until you go through Customs in Paris, but you need to be able to find it easily," Dad advised. He was twisting his bottle of water over and over in his hands.

"Need anything else?" he asked me. "Last chance for a magazine or candy bar."

"Nope. I'm all set. I have the coloring book from Isabel and my new journal from Avery, and hopefully the movie will be good."

"OK. I'll be right back. Don't board until I get back. And keep a lookout for Madame Giroux. She was going to meet us at the gate." Madame Giroux was a friend of the Morels who had been in Boston for a month and was returning to Paris on the same flight as me. Dad was glad a friend of a friend would be there to keep an eye on me.

I watched Dad jog off toward the restrooms. I had traveled to a lot of places, but never alone. Dad was by my side when we flew to Tanzania, Australia, and France and when we moved from Paris to Boston. My mom died when I was four and ever since it has been just the two of us. I loved that my dad was a travel writer. I'd been able to visit so many interesting places. We had our own special Ramsey travel contests, like racing to see who could get the most words in the airplane magazine crossword puzzle before the plane took off and seeing who would try the strangest kind of local cuisine (my dad took the lead after he ate ostrich in Tanzania).

But this time it was going to be different. I was truly on my own. And I couldn't help but be both nervous and excited at the same time.

They allowed Dad to accompany me to the gate, even though he didn't have a boarding pass, but he had to go through a million security checks. I was glad he could come—I've always loved airports because of the hustle and bustle and the people from all over the world, but they can also be pretty overwhelming. If I had to find my own way, I'd probably end up in the line for Reykjavik (Iceland) instead of Paris.

I'd been so excited about the trip that I barely slept the

night before, thinking over and over again how amazing it would be to bring Orangina home with me. I wondered what Miss Pierce would think about having a dog *and* a cat. Dad always said that we didn't find Orangina—he found us. Our first week in our houseboat on the Seine—the river that snakes its way through the middle of Paris—was in late August, and the city was steamy … much hotter than normal. The summer weather in Paris was usually pretty mild, so most Parisians didn't have air conditioning, especially in the older sections of the city. The windows were wide open and as Dad and I explored our new neighborhood, we could hear life spilling from every Parisian household.

One morning, while sitting in the white wicker chair on the back deck of the houseboat, I saw an orange glow of light in the low-lying fog. My mind raced … ghost, alien, Tinkerbell? Turned out it was a cat—an orange tabby with vibrant marmalade stripes.

"The fog comes on little cat feet," I had recited to myself as I watched the cat slink through the mist. It was the opening line of Carl Sandburg's poem "The Fog," and it described Orangina perfectly in that moment, except for one thing—Orangina wasn't little and neither were his feet.

I tried calling to him. "Shhhhh, whhhssss, whhsssss, here kitty kitty." But he glided back and forth on the bank, carefully observing the boat and me from a safe distance, and on his own terms. That's when I realized that this was not the purring, cuddly, stretch-out-and-sleep-in-the-sun type of cat. This was a cat with capital "A" attitude.

We saw him again a week later, several days after that, and then we started seeing him every day. By fall, he had warmed up to us enough that he would sleep inside the houseboat, but only by the window near the dock in case he felt like leaving in the middle of the night. I came to think of him not as a stray cat, but as MY cat. I named him Orangina, after the orange-flavored soda that's so popular in Europe. Orangina would spend hours prowling the banks of the Seine for mice. He was good at it too … we never saw a mouse on our houseboat the entire time Orangina was with us. When I would curl up on the couch to write in my journal, Orangina would watch me carefully from his favorite spot under the window. He was a true friend. So when it was time to move to the U.S., I couldn't bear to leave Paris without him.

We bought a cat carrier and were all set for the big journey. Then disaster struck. Orangina went missing!

I've always blamed Orangina's disappearance on three little boys. They were the sons of the new houseboat owners … and extremely loud and obnoxious when they came to look at the place! When the youngest one grabbed a fork off the table and chased after Orangina, that cat scrambled out the window so fast that I was sure they had scared him off for good. Turned out I was right—I never saw Orangina again after that day.

Sophie had been on the lookout for Orangina sightings ever since Dad and I left Paris, and now—finally—it seemed there was hope of seeing my lovely furball again.

My heart leapt when I heard the flight announcement. "Air France Flight 1046 for Paris now boarding first-class passengers at Gate 34." I nervously fiddled with the zipper on my messenger bag. Flying across the Atlantic without Dad was starting to seem really scary.

A mob of people in the waiting area sprang into action, gathering their belongings, but only a handful of them walked toward the gate. No matter what city, big or small, airports are the greatest places for people-watching. I think it's because people have to go to the airport for all kinds of reasons—vacation, business trip, family visit, even a mission across the Atlantic to find a lost cat. I wondered if anyone was people-watching *me*.

An Italian soccer team filed past, dressed in red warmup suits and carrying matching red duffle bags. They were laughing and talking a mile a minute.

"*Ciao, bella*! Hello beautiful!" one of the boys called to me, grinning as he passed by.

I looked down at the floor, a little embarrassed, but also kind of flattered that I had been called "beautiful." Maeve would swoon when I told her—she thought Italian boys were dreamy.

My eyes wandered over to the other side of the terminal where a family was packing up their carry-on bags. A little girl with blond pigtails ran up and down the row of seats with a miniature pink rolling suitcase. She tripped on its wheels and tumbled to the floor. Her mother picked her up, suitcase and all, and sat her between her two brothers, who were so engrossed in their video games that they didn't seem to hear their sister's snuffling.

Nearby, an annoyed older man looked up from his newspaper, picked up his leather briefcase, and moved to the far end of the seats. A small group of women in matching red hats knitted quietly. A college boy with curly hair practiced tricks with a yo-yo, flinging it dangerously close to several people as they hurried past with their luggage. I could have filled a whole journal with descriptions of the people around me. I wondered about their stories … where they came from, where they were going, and what they were all about.

I spotted Dad jogging toward me as a voice sounded over the loudspeaker.

"Any passengers traveling with small children or anyone needing special assistance …" The Air France employee announced instructions for the next group to board the plane. I shot a warning look at Dad before he sent me toward the gate with the 3 and 4 year olds.

"OK, I get it. You're not a little girl. You'll always be *my* little girl, though," he said, and then swallowed hard. "Now, you be careful … and don't talk to any strangers. Madame Giroux will be there if you have any problems on the flight. Speaking of … where is Madame Giroux? She's supposed to be meeting us right here."

Just then, Dad's cell phone began to ring. "Hello?" he answered and stepped into a quieter corner to take the call.

"Madame Giroux is stuck in security," Dad announced after he flipped his phone shut and joined me again. "She says to go ahead and board the plane ... she'll meet you at your seat."

"OK," I agreed, trying not to show Dad how nervous I was.

"I'm going to miss you, you know. It'll be strange this week to come home from work to an empty house." Dad looked so sad that I thought for a moment I might cry. I tried to chase the tears away by forcing a smile.

"Come on, Dad," I said, gently slugging his shoulder. "You won't really be alone. Marty will take care of you. And Miss Pierce is right downstairs. Just think—you can turn up those jazz tunes as loud as you want and eat sardines, anchovies, and all those smelly fish dishes that make me gag."

Dad laughed, but it wasn't a big, happy laugh. When they called my row number, I hugged Dad extra tight. He and I were a team. It was hard to leave him. Choking back a sob, I broke away.

"Call me as soon as you get to Sophie's. I love you."

"I love you too." I waved at Dad as I joined the line of people waiting to walk down the jetway. The flight attendant smiled as I handed my boarding pass to her. "Good evening, *mademoiselle. Bon voyage.*"

"*Bonsoir. Merci,*" I replied as I took the boarding pass back and carefully put it into the smallest pocket of my bag. Walking backward down the jetway, I waved good-bye to

Dad, who was still anxiously peering through the crowd.

"Love you," I mouthed just before bumping into the couple in front of me, who had stopped suddenly. After apologizing and picking up a small pillow the woman dropped, I tried to catch another glimpse of Dad but only saw the top of his head. Before I knew it, I reached the door of the plane. I was off to Paris, and on my own for the first time ever. I gulped back the lump in my throat, stifled a squeak of excitement, and stepped aboard the plane.

Hi BSGs!

I'm on my way
to Paris,
and I miss you
already!

Your BFF,
Charlotte

PS Thanks for all of the
wonderful gifts!

PPS Give Marty a special
treat from me!

III

Comme un Rêve

JUST LIKE A DREAM

"WELCOME ABOARD Air France Flight 1046, nonstop service to Charles de Gaulle International Airport. This is your captain, Sébastien Naiseux speaking. We hope to be in the air in about twenty minutes. We are so fortunate this evening; the weather report is clear all across the Atlantic. We can expect an early 9 a.m. arrival in the famous City of Light. So sit back, relax, and enjoy the flight. *Bienvenue à bord* Flight 1046 ..."

As I listened to the message repeated in French, I gripped the cushioned armrest of my seat in the middle row. I almost had to pinch myself. I just couldn't believe that I, Charlotte Ramsey, was actually flying all alone to see my best Paris friend, Sophie, and to hunt for Orangina.

All around me, passengers were settling down, pulling books and newspapers out of their carry-ons and half watching the flight attendants demonstrate safety procedures. My heart raced as I clipped my seatbelt into its metal catch. Paris, my wonderful Paris. I could smell its sweet *parfum* already!

I couldn't wait for the plane to take off. To keep myself busy, I reached into the messenger bag sandwiched between my feet to dig out my new journal and pen, But when I tried to shove the bag under the seat it got stuck. I braced my foot against the plane floor and tugged as hard as I could. *Ugh* ... Suddenly, the bag popped forward, sending me back against my seat. My glasses slid down my nose and the contents of my bag rolled under the seat. *Oh no, not AGAIN!* I thought, closing my eyes. Hopefully no one had seen the World's Biggest Klutz have yet another one of her classic moments.

"Bonjour ma chérie! You must be Charlotte." I looked up to see a very pretty woman in a cream-colored suit smiling down at me. She had a major twinkle in her eye. I admired how sophisticated she looked and was embarrassed that she had witnessed my backpack spaz-attack just now. "I am Madame Giroux," she told me.

"Oh, of course!" I exclaimed. I struggled to stand up in the tiny seat to properly shake her hand. I reached out and said, "Nice to meet you, Madame." But Madame Giroux didn't shake my hand. Instead she kissed me on one cheek, then the other, then the first cheek again, then the other cheek. I couldn't believe I had forgotten the traditional French greeting—*la bise*, the quadruple kiss!

Madame Giroux gracefully took the seat to my right, placing her white leather purse at her feet and then picking it up again to remove a tube of deep, red lipstick. No bags burst open. No glasses slid. *Incredible!* I thought. *Just how DO French women manage to be so graceful in any situation?* Madame Giroux wasn't even the least bit flustered that she was so late getting to her seat.

"Pardon me, ladies, but I believe this is my seat … 23E?" said a voice in a dignified British accent. I watched as the man cheerfully stuffed his luggage into the overhead compartment and sat down in the aisle seat to my left.

He was an older gentleman with thick, snow-white hair, a trim white mustache, and very kind eyes. He wore a brown tweed jacket and a crisp white shirt, which made him look like some sort of proper professor type.

Maybe he's a famous archeologist flying to Paris, then on to Egypt to study a secret hieroglyphic message someone just found on a tomb of some ancient Egyptian king or queen. Oops! There I go again. When I'm traveling, I tend to get carried away imagining all kinds of exotic things. My dad says that being imaginative is a very good quality for an aspiring writer to have.

"Harold? Harold Peckham?" gasped Madame Giroux. "I cannot believe my eyes!"

"Good heavens! Amelie! You look magnificent!" Madame stood up and they quadruple-kissed each other hello. It was so very French of them.

"Charlotte," Madame Giroux said, turning to me as she sat down again, "this is a dear old friend of mine, the *formidable* Harold Peckham. He owns the most authentic

English pub in Paris! It is one of my restaurants favorites!"
I smiled. Madame Giroux had mixed up her sentence with
English and French. I chuckled, figuring I would be doing
a lot of that in the next week.

Mr. Peckham laughed modestly. It was a soft laugh,
rich and kind.

"Hello," I murmured. I was still wrestling to get all
my scattered things back into my bag and in the correct
position for takeoff.

"Might I assist you, miss?" Mr. Peckham asked politely
in a very proper British accent.

I pushed my glasses back into place and smiled
gratefully. "Thanks. I guess I stuffed it too full this time.
Would you mind putting it in the overhead bin for me?"

"Why, of course not," he said, carefully stowing my
bag above.

"Harold G. Peckham, Esquire, at your service," he
declared and bowed deeply, bumping his head on an
armrest as he straightened up.

Now it was my turn to laugh. Either my klutziness was
contagious, or Mr. Peckham was clumsy too. "I'm Charlotte
Ramsey. It's very nice to meet you, Mr. Peckham."

Mr. Peckham and I both sat back down, and I opened
up my new journal and uncapped my pen. This was going
to be a wonderful trip, I just knew it! I closed my eyes and
listened to the noises surrounding me. Ms. Rodriguez, the
advisor to *The Sentinel*, always said, "*Details*. You must
capture your readers with lots and lots of *details*." Since I

intended to become a writer (and hopefully a good one) someday, I tried to practice observing the sights and sounds of my surroundings. It could be a lot of fun once you got into it.

For example, as the plane prepared for takeoff, I could hear bins slamming shut, a baby crying, flight attendants checking to make sure that everyone buckled their seatbelts, a little boy asking if we were in Paris yet, a woman telling the person next to her that she was afraid to fly, and a man talking on a cell phone to his broker ... something about, "Harry, I demand that you get me out of that ridiculous stock now. I can't believe I let you talk me into buying shares in a company that sells Christmas trees to Russia." Suddenly, an announcement came over the loudspeaker asking that everyone return to their seats and turn off cell phones and other "electronic devices." We were almost ready to depart from the gate.

As the plane began inching slowly toward the runway, I stared out the window to see if I could catch a glimpse of Dad. These past couple of days had been such a blur. This was my first chance to slow down and write about everything that led up to my *voyage incroyable* to my old home.

"We wound our way in and out of the small cobblestone streets of the historic Fifth Arrondissement . . ."

~ pg. 53

Charlotte's Journal

I've spent so many nights looking out my window, staring up at the constellation Orion, dreaming of Paris. I will never forget the vision of the Eiffel Tower all lit up, twinkling at nighttime, the houseboat that Dad and I lived in on the River Seine before we moved to Boston, or my cat, Orangina, who ran away right before we moved. And how could I ever forget my friend Sophie?

Paris feels like it's MY city. It's a place where everything comes alive. I still remember it all so clearly — the musical sound of the French language, the fragrance of the most amazing fresh pastries, the aroma of rich coffee, climbing up the staircase of the métro and standing right in front of the Arc de Triomphe. It feels like just yesterday that Sophie and I were walking across the Pont Royal, exploring the sights and sounds of the city together.

I really cannot wait to see ma copine Sophie again. We email all the time, but it's not the same as talking face to face. Sophie was my best friend in Paris, and I only survived my first days in Boston because I had Sophie's emails to read when I came home from school. Though I'm happy to have a real home in Brookline, and I wouldn't trade it for anything else in the world, Paris will always have a special place in my heart.

★

I sighed as I put my journal down. It was hard to believe everything that had happened in the last few days. It seemed like I had left Dad at the gate a week ago instead of forty-five minutes ago.

I heard something rattling and turned around to see one of the flight attendants pushing a cart. The phrase "What would you like to drink?" was repeated over and over again as he briskly shook juices, filled little plastic cups with ice, and handed over soda cans and miniature wine bottles.

"I'll have a glass of tomato juice, please, and what would you like, young lady?" Mr. Peckham asked me.

"Orange juice, please."

The flight attendant handed over our drinks with tiny bags of pretzels. Madame Giroux requested a bottle of sparkling water.

"Is this your first trip to Paris?" Mr. Peckham asked as he poured his juice into a plastic cup.

As we sipped our drinks, the whole story about my father's job, our houseboat on the Seine, Sophie, and Orangina poured out. Mr. Peckham listened intently, asking questions about the confusing parts and laughing at the right times.

"How long have you lived in Paris?" I asked Mr. Peckham. As the flight attendants made their way down the aisles with the dinner carts, "Chicken or beef?" "Chicken or beef?" "Chicken or beef?" was starting to sound like a really bad, never-ending jingle.

"Oh my, since I was just a young lad," Mr. Peckham explained. "I was born and raised in a tiny hamlet on the northeast coast of England. Staithes is just north of Whitby near the York Moors. Its only claim to fame is that it was Captain Cook's—you know, the famous explorer— boyhood town. I first visited Paris when I was about your age with my parents. When I was seventeen I moved there and it has been my home ever since." He sliced his beef into near-perfect strips with his plastic knife.

"Do you miss England?" I asked, digging into my mashed potatoes and carrots. I was starving, so everything tasted OK, even though the airplane food was far from gourmet.

"Oh, not too much, my dear. Staithes, I understand, hasn't changed a bit since I first left. I visited a few times while my mum was still alive, but I haven't been back in over a decade. For the past forty years, I have been the proprietor of the Churchill Pub. It's the most authentic English pub in Paris and London, too, if I *do* say so myself. I would wager that I have made more friends in that pub than I ever would have if I stayed in Staithes. Lovely people like Madame Giroux, here. She stops by for dinner at least once each week."

"*Mais oui*! But of course I do!" Madame Giroux said. "You have the best fish and chips in all of Paris."

"Thank you, my dear. Anyway, I'm happy leading the life of an expatriate," Mr. Peckham declared. "Paris has a certain *je ne sais quoi*—a special quality that is hard to describe. It's a city that can make the old feel young again and make the young wise beyond their years." I knew he was talking about me. I was really flattered that Mr. Peckham thought I seemed wise.

Madame Giroux pulled a novel from her bag. "I don't like to fly, and reading relaxes me," she confided. "If you need anything, Charlotte, just ask me OK?" I was too excited to relax. Luckily Mr. Peckham liked to chat.

He pointed to my arm. "I am very intrigued by your bracelets. What a wonderful collection you have!"

"Oh, thanks!" I looked down at the assortment of colors that decorated my wrist. I was relieved that Madame Giroux seemed absorbed in her book. My bracelets were really meaningful to me, but they weren't exactly sophisticated or *chic*, and certainly nothing that a fashionable woman from Paris would ever wear.

"I have a feeling each bracelet has its own story," Mr. Peckham said, his eyes crinkling as he smiled. "Did you collect them yourself, or were they gifts?"

"Sophie—my friend that I'm going to visit in Paris—helped me make the hemp one. The neon orange one is something I picked up at the *marché aux puces*."

"One might find anything imaginable at the flea market, am I right?"

I nodded. "The green malachite is from a market in Tanzania. And my favorite is from Australia. It's made of sea glass."

"Australia! You don't say," Mr. Peckham exclaimed.

"We lived in Port Douglas when Dad was working on a book about the Great Barrier Reef. I love sea glass. I used to walk along the shore to find bits of glass that were shaped and polished by years of traveling the ocean."

"Travel certainly does expand one's perspective," Mr. Peckham commented.

"Yes. I guess it's kind of silly to wear so many bracelets that don't match, but they remind me of all the places that I've been to."

"I don't think it's silly at all," Mr. Peckham said as he reached inside his jacket pocket. He pulled out a set of keys, detached the key chain, and placed it on the tray in front of me. I picked it up to examine it more closely. It was a perfect four-leaf clover preserved forever in a bubble of plastic.

"I've been presented with far more elegant key chains, but this one has a place in my heart and in my pocket. It was my mum's. She gave it to me when I was just a lad, and just seeing it every day gives me comfort and grand memories of her."

I smiled as I thought of my mom's denim jacket and the copy of *Charlotte's Web* that she used to read to me. I kept them near me as treasured memories of my own mom. It seemed that Mr. Peckham and I had quite a bit in common after all.

"Are you an art fan as well?" Mr. Peckham asked me, pointing to the Picasso coloring book as he put his keys back on the key chain.

I hoped Mr. Peckham didn't think the coloring book was childish. "My friend Isabel is a huge art fan, and an artist, too. She loves Picasso. She gave me this book to teach me a little more about his artwork."

"Charming fellow, Picasso. You know, I actually met the chap once."

"Picasso? You mean THE Pablo Picasso?" Isabel would just die when I told her that I had met someone who had met Picasso!

"Oh, yes. It was many, many years ago, of course. Decades ago in fact. When I was just a young whipper-snapper. He came into the pub a few times. Remarkable man. Stupendous talent. I even saw him make a few sketches. Nothing fancy ... just charcoal sketches on the back of his bar bills. But in those few lines he was able to capture the very essence of his subject." He paused and stared off into space as if reliving the moment.

Mr. Peckham thoughtfully smoothed his mustache and cleared his throat. "Will you be able to visit any museums while you are in Paris?"

"Uh ... well ... I don't know. I think we'll spend most of our time searching for Orangina. And I'm not sure if the Morels have anything planned."

"Do you have a picture of your missing feline? I will keep my eyes open for the cat if I know what to look for," promised Mr. Peckham.

I reached into my wallet and pulled out my snapshots.

Mr. Peckham examined a small photo of Orangina

sunbathing on the docks. "Orangina is certainly an appropriate name for this spectacular orange creature!" Then he pointed to a picture of Marty. "Who is this little fellow, might I ask?"

"This is my dog, Marty. My friends and I found him abandoned in a park near my house. Do you think it's weird to carry around pictures of pets in your wallet?"

Mr. Peckham's mustache twitched and a smile lit up his face as he pulled his wallet from his chest pocket. "I carry a picture of my pooch as well. A black Scottish terrier by the name of Wellington. A rather grand name for a canine, is it not? I think it had rather gone to his head. Even if he was really only named after rubber boots that keep out the English rain. He was terribly spoiled. See that smug little look on his face?" Mr. Peckham asked as he showed me a cracked black-and-white photo of the most adorable Scottie in a plaid doggie sweater. He did look a little spoiled. Next to the picture of the dog was a picture of a beautiful, dark-haired woman in a flowing dress.

"This woman is so beautiful. Is she your wife?" I asked.

Mr. Peckham pulled the picture out and gazed at it thoughtfully. He took a long, deep breath and let it out slowly. "I had hoped she would be …" he said with a heavy sigh. "But alas … she married someone else. Ah, unrequited love …" he sighed, clutching his heart.

"Oh … I'm sorry. I didn't mean to pry …"

"It was hard enough to lose her, but then she married that awful man …"

✤

I felt bad that I had brought up the subject and made Mr. Peckham upset.

"Do you ever see her?" I asked gently, hoping the story had a happy ending.

"No ... I hadn't seen Agnes in decades. Then last June, she died."

All I could say was, "I'm sorry."

"She deserved to marry someone who appreciated her exquisite beauty ... her charming character. But instead she married a terrible cad who was incapable of appreciating anything."

Mr. Peckham stopped. He seemed flustered and sad. He lowered his head so he could look out the window past the seats to his left.

I opened up my journal again and stared at the seat back in front of me, trying to sort through my thoughts before picking up my pen. Maeve would love this story. She was fascinated by tragic romances of any kind.

Charlotte's Journal

Poor Mr. Peckham. To lose the love of one's life. He seems so sad. It's such a change from the talkative, friendly gentleman he was just a few minutes ago. I wish I could say something to make him feel better ... or turn back time and not have asked so many questions. If I could have one super power, I would want to be a time traveler. It's so easy to make mistakes that it'd be great if it was just as easy to go back and fix them.

I wonder what the real story is behind the dark-haired

woman and the man who stole her away. It seems like she was a really important part of Mr. Peckham's life. Maeve would definitely think this whole thing was SO romantic. Note: Why is it that on planes strangers seem to open up and tell you things they'd never reveal in the supermarket checkout line?

Right now there is a movie playing on the plane, but I've already seen it, so I just have headphones on for some background noise. Mr. Peckham and Madame Giroux are both sound asleep. Madame Giroux has a fancy neck pillow, ear plugs, and even an eye mask to keep the light out. But somehow she just looks really peaceful, not ridiculous, with all of her travel accessories.

The further we get across the Atlantic (I keep looking at the map and the timetable in the airline magazine!), the more real this trip becomes. I absolutely cannot wait to land, walk into the airport, and be surrounded by everything French. And I can't wait to see Sophie! There's so much I want to talk to her about! My new house, my friends, the Tower, Nick ... I hope she and I will be as close as we used to be. What if she's more grown up than me and thinks that I'm immature? She seems like the same old funny, kind Sophie in all of her emails and letters, though. But you never know. Things change.

My eyes started feeling really heavy. I checked my watch ... almost 11 p.m. ... 5 a.m. Paris time. I stuck the little white pillow under my head and closed my eyes.

★

✦

I woke up to a familiar rattling noise. My head had slid to the right, just inches from Madame Giroux's shoulder. I sat up quickly, checking to make sure I hadn't drooled on her beautiful blouse. It would have been mortifying to say, "That glop on your shirt would be from me. I hope you don't mind."

"Well, Miss Charlotte!" Mr. Peckham bellowed, as upbeat as ever. "You're just in time for breakfast." He gestured to the plastic tray in front of me.

I couldn't believe it when my watch said 2:10 a.m. Had I switched the time? Paris was six hours ahead of Boston. "I wasn't asleep for three hours, was I?" I asked.

"Indeed you were! I expect you must have been exhausted from the whirlwind of travel preparations," Mr. Peckham explained. "That always happens to me."

"Boy, I guess I'd better change my watch," I said. I adjusted the hands and smiled. We only had another hour or so left!

After finishing his tea, Mr. Peckham peered across the aisle and through the window. "Our long journey's end is in sight. Perhaps I should visit the loo before we land. Will you excuse me?" Mr. Peckham unbuckled his seatbelt, got to his feet, shook out his legs, and headed to the back of the plane. Loo is such a wonderful word, so much more polite sounding than *bathroom*, I thought.

I looked out the window. I could hardly believe it! We'd flown over the entire Atlantic Ocean! I glanced at Madame Giroux to my right. She looked very much like the illustration of Sleeping Beauty—if Sleeping Beauty had an eye mask and ear plugs. I couldn't help but hope that some of the Parisian sophistication and style would rub off on me this week. Not that I wanted to change completely, but a little style never hurt anyone, Katani was fond of saying.

After Mr. Peckham returned, the pilot made an announcement that we would be landing soon. Madame Giroux awoke and checked her appearance in a small silver compact. "We're almost there Charlotte!" She smiled brightly. I nodded my head and squeezed out a tired smile. She was the picture of poise. How could that be? I wondered. Maybe it was the French food that made people so stylish. I, on the other hand, was hot, crumpled, and wrinkly from sitting in such a cramped space for so long. I hoped with all my might I'd be able to remember enough French to communicate with the locals.

The plane touched down, and for the second time that day I felt as if there were a gazillion butterflies racing around my stomach. I kept telling myself that we were in France, but I could hardly believe it. As we taxied to the gate, blue lights flashed and odd-sounding European sirens wailed as police cars went zooming past our plane.

"My, my," Mr. Peckham murmured, trying to see the activity out the window.

"Do you think there's a problem at the airport?" I asked.

"Not to worry," Madame Giroux reassured us. "Just because you see police at the airport doesn't necessarily mean there is a real emergency. Paris police are cracking down on all sorts of crimes. Just last week, they arrested a jewel thief trying to smuggle jewels into the country. They were waiting for him in the terminal when he got off the plane. With such high security these days, most criminals don't have a chance!"

Mr. Peckham jumped to his feet as soon as the seatbelt sign was turned off. "Allow me to help you gather your things," he said to me. Passengers were crowding around the overhead bins, eager to pull down their bags and be on their way.

I handed Mr. Peckham the Picasso coloring book, colored pencil bag, and my journal, and placed the Morels' gift basket on my seat. I'd been so entertained by him during the flight that I hadn't even glanced at Isabel's gift, let alone colored in the book. Mr. Peckham put my things into my messenger bag and then lowered it from the bin to my seat.

"What part of Paris is your final destination?" Mr. Peckham asked as we waited to get off the plane.

"Oh, we'll be spending time all over the city," I answered vaguely. Even though I liked Mr. Peckham very much, and he seemed like a nice man, I was careful not to tell him exactly where I was staying in the city. How could I forget Dad's "be careful of strangers" lecture that he had given me every night before I left? He always said that when you are a world traveler you have to follow certain "safety precautions."

"Very nice," Mr. Peckham said distractedly.

"Are you all right?" I asked. Mr. Peckham's face was suddenly very red—almost purple—and his forehead was beaded with sweat.

He took a handkerchief from his pocket and dabbed at his forehead.

"Yes. Quite. How kind of you to ask. It's been a long flight, and it's just a little stuffy in here, don't you think?" He cleared his throat and looked anxiously at the rows of people that still had to exit before we could.

It seemed to take forever for us to shuffle from the plane down the long, crowded jetway. Conversations in French bombarded me from every direction as we headed toward Customs. I understood most of what I heard, but would I be able to speak French myself? I just hoped that people wouldn't look at me like I had three heads when I started talking to them.

Mr. Peckham and Madame Giroux stayed by my side as we waited in the long line at Customs, claimed our baggage, and finally made our way through the security area. The moment we were cleared through, Mr. Peckham put on his coat and hat.

"Well, I must be on my way ... I wish you a splendid trip, Charlotte, and lots of good luck finding your feline. I'm sure I'll be seeing you soon, Amelie," he said, turning to tip his hat to Madame Giroux.

Mr. Peckham was already halfway to the airport exit before I could respond, "Good-bye, Mr. Peckham. So nice talking to you!"

"Charlotte! *Ma chérie!*"

Her voice was just as lively as I remembered it. I turned and saw Sophie hurrying toward me, her father a few steps behind.

I suddenly felt a little shy. I walked toward Sophie and gave her a little wave and looked down. A wave? What was I thinking? As if she were just an acquaintance I was passing on the street! Sophie returned the wave with a huge smile and a laugh, which made me feel less awkward.

"Oh Charlotte … you are exactly the same! I'm so glad!" Sophie hugged me before giving me *la bise*, those four little kisses on alternating cheeks. Before I knew it, French was flying out of my mouth, and I was telling Sophie how glad I was to see her and how excited I was to be in France again at last.

Monsieur Morel, who had been chatting with Madame Giroux, turned to us. "Well, girls, would you like to spend your week together in the airport, or shall we go home? I know Jacqueline is anxious to see that you have arrived safely."

"Let's go," I grinned and turned to say good-bye to Madame Giroux. "Thank you so much, Madame."

"*Je t'en prie*, it's nothing, Charlotte. *Au revoir* … I hope you have a wonderful trip." Madame waved as she made her way to the airport exit.

I was wide awake, even after the long journey— exhilarated with the joy of seeing Sophie. As we walked

"I can't believe I'm really here!" ~ pg. 53

❧

outside to catch a taxi, I began asking Sophie about what had happened in the months I'd been away. Suddenly, it all came flooding back—exciting times with Sophie exploring the streets of Paris seemed like just yesterday.

~ IV ~

Vive La Différence

HERE'S TO OUR DIFFERENCES

"I CAN'T BELIEVE I'M REALLY HERE!" I exclaimed as the taxi bumped along. I gazed out the window at the familiar buildings that lined the streets. We had finally made our way into the city itself, and I was trying to take in everything at once. It was just after 10 a.m. Paris time, but it felt like it should be much earlier since it was only 4 a.m. back in Boston. We wound our way in and out of the small cobblestone streets of the historic Fifth Arrondissement, a lively section of Paris full of restaurants, bookstores, and lovely parks.

"You are the same Charlotte, but somehow you seem more ... American!" Sophie observed me carefully as I gazed out the window.

"I was always American," I reminded her.

"*Mais oui*! But you were an American coming from Australia. Now it is in the way you dress ... the ski jacket, the running shoes, the bag. It's always easy to pick out the

American tourists by their clothes. But you are not a tourist ... you've come home!"

I smiled and glanced out the window again. It felt good to hear Sophie say that I'd come home. I think people can be at home in many different places ... Paris just happened to be one of mine.

"Have you seen Orangina since I last spoke to you?" I asked Sophie.

"No, I returned to the quay yesterday afternoon, but *rien* ... nothing," Sophie waved her hand. "Don't worry, *mon amie*, we will search everywhere this week. He's alive and well, we know that for sure now. I am certain that I saw him ... there is no mistaking that *boule de fourrure orange*—that orange furball. But he will only come to you ... you know how stubborn he is."

"Do I ever!" I agreed. "Remember when I stepped on his tail by mistake and then he refused to come back onto the houseboat, even though it was pouring rain? He just sat outside the door glaring for an entire day."

The taxi squeaked to a halt in front of the Morels' apartment house on rue Jacob. "*Nous sommes arrivés,*" said Monsieur Morel. "Here we are."

As we got out of the taxi, I noticed that Sophie, too, looked different, although I couldn't pinpoint what it was. She was taller, and her hair was swept up and twisted into a small clip, with a few pieces framing her face. She wore fitted jeans, a white camisole top, a black off-the-shoulder sweater, and tall black boots. Was it the clothes? Was it the way she lifted her chin? Or was it that confident sparkle in her eyes?

Was this a new, more sophisticated Sophie that I had not seen before? Or was it just my imagination?

"Here we are!" Sophie echoed her father.

I looked up at the apartment house. Miss Pierce's Victorian on Corey Hill seemed old, but by Paris standards, it was practically brand new. The Morels' building was ancient, but it was renovated and very fancy. We took the elevator to the eighth floor and then walked the spiral staircase to the Morels' rooftop apartment, where through the windows the whole of Paris was spread out before us.

Madame Morel was waiting at the door. Sophie's mom greeted me *"en français."* *"Bonjour*! Oh, Charlotte, you've come back to us at last! It's wonderful to see you. Welcome home!" Again the hug and *la bise* left me feeling like a true Parisian. "You must be *très fatiguée* from your journey. We will give you a moment to catch your breath and unpack your clothes. But hurry back and we will have some hot food. That airplane food is not even fit for a dog!" Madame Morel was so particular about her food. In fact, I couldn't wait to have one of her great French meals. "After we eat, you must have a long rest and then you will feel like yourself again." I couldn't help but remember my father's description of Madame Morel as a "marathon talker."

I handed Sophie's mother the plastic bag containing the gift basket of homemade treats from Montoya's. *"Voilà —* here you go! This is for you, for having me in Paris. Now you can taste the pastries from Boston," I told Madame Morel as she looked at the basket with pleasant surprise.

"*Merci*, Charlotte. You didn't have to do this," she said, giving me another hug. "Now you two run along and freshen up."

Sophie grabbed my hand and led me to her room.

After I splashed some cold water on my face, I arranged my clothes in the drawer that Sophie always used to clear out for me. Sophie was a bit like Katani—very neat and organized. She had hangers ready for me, my bed was turned down, and she had even left a chocolate by my bedside. She said she was practicing for when she had her own hotel.

"Just imagine, Charlotte. Hotel Sophie splashed across the entry. You will always be welcome, and I will have a room called Charlotte's Room. We will have a telescope and lavender in the pots and a portrait of Orangina and your little doggie on the wall."

I had forgotten how imaginative Sophie was. I could feel myself getting carried away with her dream.

"Where will Hotel Sophie be?" I asked. "You know, I will be traveling around the world, so I hope it will be in a very restful place."

"*Mais alors*, Charlotte. Have you already forgotten my favorite spot in the world?"

"The Côte d'Azur," I smiled broadly. How could I forget Sophie's favorite summer vacation spot?

"Yes, I will have the most *chic* spot on ze beach. My

American convertible T-Bird will be parked in the courtyard and there will be chocolate everywhere."

For the next half hour, Sophie and I planned Hotel Sophie down to every detail. We had one mini argument about what kind of chocolates to serve at breakfast because both Sophie and I were chocolate fanatics and could get very insistent about our preferences.

When Madame Morel called us in for breakfast, I stood for a moment in front of the Morels' living room window. The view from their apartment was truly amazing. Floor-to-ceiling windows on one whole living room wall overlooked the city. I had a rooftop view that could have been a Paris postcard.

Ah, Paris. The very air seemed alive. Not like the electric energy and hustle bustle of New York or Boston, but truly alive. It was as if every moment, every breath was precious, and the city was coaxing me to slow down and appreciate it. I felt so lucky to be here with my friends once again.

"Come Charlotte. *Le petit-déjeuner est prêt*—breakfast is ready!" Sophie smiled as she linked her arm through mine and led me into the dining room.

Madame Morel had set out fresh croissants from the bakery, a colorful fruit salad of grapes, melon, and strawberries, and eggs baked with cheese and tomatoes. She took my plate and served me small portions of everything. Super-sizing was not a French custom. Perhaps that was one reason the French looked so trim and fit. Madame Morel poured me a steaming mug of hot chocolate and a glass of ice water as well.

I waited until everyone else had filled their plates and then eagerly tasted everything. The memories came back with every bite I took.

"Were you frightened to be traveling on your own?" Madame Morel asked.

"I wasn't really on my own. Madame Giroux was right beside me the whole time. And we ran into a friend of hers on the plane—a Mr. Peckham. I spent a lot of the flight talking to him. He was nice, but he had the most tragic love story to tell!"

Suddenly, Sophie clapped eagerly, catching everyone's attention. "Charlotte, everyone at school is so happy you've come back to visit. When I told the class on Thursday, the students didn't stop talking about it all day!" Sophie's eyes sparkled with excitement.

"Really?" I was surprised. "I haven't been so very good at keeping in touch with anyone but you. I kind of thought everyone might have forgotten about me by now."

"How could you think they would forget *you*, Charlotte?" Sophie wondered, elegantly sipping her hot chocolate. "You live in America. Everyone wants to hear about your adventures. They all want to know if you've ever seen Tom Cruise or Natalie Portman."

I smiled as I took a bite of my croissant and wiped the buttery flakes off my chin. This was why I loved being a world traveler. I've learned that there are amazing people everywhere, and now here I was ready to see my old classmates again.

After we finished our meal, Madame Morel insisted that I sleep for a while, even though I was reluctant to waste even one moment of my visit.

"We will leave you in peace for a few hours, and there will still be much of the day left for exploring," Madame Morel gently assured me.

Sophie and I went back to her room. I loved how it was decorated all in cream and deep rosy magenta. Very sophisticated, I thought. As I took off my sneakers and crawled into the roll-away bed the Morels set up for me, I reminded myself to describe it to Katani. Sophie sat down at her desk and took out her schoolbooks.

"I'm going to study as much as I can until you wake up. If I can get ahead on my assignments, then this week will be like a vacation for *moi aussi* ... me too!" Sophie quietly began to read and write in her notebook.

Despite my earlier protests, I found my eyelids getting heavy. Just as I was about to drift off, I bolted upright.

"What is it?" Sophie asked, startled at my sudden burst of energy.

"I forgot to call my dad!" I exclaimed, hopping out of bed. "Is it OK if I use the phone in the hallway? My dad got me an international calling card to pay for long-distance calls."

"*Bien sûr*! Of course!" Sophie said, gesturing toward the door.

✦

I found the calling card in my wallet and took it with me into the hallway.

"Charlotte?" Dad sounded tired when he answered the phone.

"Hi, Dad. I'm here. I'm sorry I forgot to call earlier," I said quickly.

"It's OK, Char. I'm glad you finally remembered, though. I was getting worried, but then I checked online and saw that your flight landed safely, so I decided to wait a little while before checking up on you. How is everything going?"

"It's amazing, Dad. I can't believe I'm back here. It's just like I remembered it … almost as if I never left. I was afraid that I wouldn't remember my French, but it's coming back to me no problem."

"That's great, kiddo. Have fun and be careful, OK? Say hello to Sophie and the Morels. And don't forget to eat some *escargots* for me."

How could I forget? Snails—no one in America understood how tasty snails could be all smothered in butter and garlic. Yum! I smacked my lips.

"Bye, Dad. Love you … and thanks so much for letting me do this."

"You're welcome, Char. Love you too. Remember to keep a journal now."

I hung up the phone, went back into Sophie's room, and crawled into the bed all over again.

"Good night, Sophie," I said.

"Good *morning*, Charlotte," Sophie replied, pointing to the clock.

I giggled and then snuggled into the soft comforter and drifted off to sleep.

★

When I woke up, the sun was shining brightly through the gaps between the shade and the window. It took a moment to realize where I was, and I grinned as the events of the past day came flooding back.

I hopped out of bed, smoothed the comforter into place, and quickly tied on my running shoes. I found Sophie in the kitchen, stirring a big pot of soup.

"Hello, sleepyhead. You were asleep for almost four hours. Did you have a good rest?" Sophie asked.

"Yup, I did. I guess I needed it. Can I help you in here?"

"Nonsense!" said Madame Morel. "You girls go enjoy the rest of the afternoon. Just make sure you are back by 7 o'clock for dinner."

Sophie and I put on our coats and went out into the brisk air. It would have been chilly if the sun wasn't shining so brightly. We walked away from the Seine up rue Jacob and headed to the nearby Jardin du Luxembourg, one of our favorite places in the city. The park was filled with families, joggers, and couples enjoying the sunny afternoon. Everyone in Paris loved the Jardin.

"Remember when we took my little cousins to the merry-go-round here last spring? Adèle refused to come down from the horse when the ride was over," Sophie laughed as she recalled that afternoon.

I giggled. "You had to drag her off the horse while she was kicking and screaming. And then we took them for ice cream at La Buvette des Marionnettes and Claude dropped his ice cream and wanted to take his spoon and eat it off the ground. I'm so glad we're not baby-sitting today."

After walking slowly through the park for an hour, we stopped at an *épicerie* and bought a *baguette* and a package of herb cheese from the grocer. We sat on a bench outside the store, tore off pieces of the bread, and dipped it in the cheese. Dinner was in about an hour, but since neither of us could wait that long, we decided to treat ourselves to a little *amuse gueule*—an appetizer. It would be about lunchtime now back at home. Maeve would adore Paris, I thought. All of the couples walking by were holding hands and staring into each other's eyes. So romantic.

"I suppose we should head back now … *Maman* will be annoyed if we're late. She's been planning this dinner for three days!" Sophie brushed a few crumbs off her jeans as she stood up, and in a moment we were off, giggling through *les rues de Paris*—the streets of Paris—as though I'd never left.

Dinner was absolutely spectacular. I felt like I was at the Ritz—the Paris Ritz. All white linen, roses, candles, silver, and china. Monsieur Morel lit a fire in the dining room fireplace. The flames crackled on one side of me while the lights of Paris sparkled on the other. Madame Morel brought in each course from the kitchen—a simple, but elegant meal. We started with a small bowl of her famous sorrel soup, full of delicious leafy greens, onions, and potatoes. I inhaled it. Madame Morel was very pleased.

Dad and I cooked together all the time, but our dinners were pretty informal, and we gobbled up the food in no time. I think it's part of the fast-paced American life. Watching the Morels eat was like watching a ballet. Every movement was graceful. Conversation bubbled around me. Madame Morel, who worked at La Samaritaine, one of the largest department stores in Paris, told me all about her new job, and Sophie filled me in on the latest gossip from school. I tried not to slurp or spill the delicious soup as I listened intently.

After the entrée—beef *bourguignon*—came the cheese tray. Monsieur Morel was a cheese exporter. He explained to me that a proper cheese tray has a variety of milks (cow's, goat's, and sheep's) as well as a variety of textures (soft, medium, and hard) … the variety makes the whole experience pleasing for the taste buds and the palate. He carefully carved tiny slices of cheese for me to sample. My favorite was the *Doux de Montagne*. It was delicious …

✦

creamy, nutty, and buttery all at once.

When we'd all tried the different cheeses, Madame Morel took the cheese tray back to the kitchen and returned with *crème brûlé* for dessert.

"Oh, this is my favorite dessert in the world!" I exclaimed as I spied the custard with the burnt sugar caramel on top.

"But of course, Charlotte ... I remembered how you loved it, but Sophie made sure to remind me just in case," smiled Madame Morel.

After dessert, Madame Morel served espresso to the adults. Sophie went to a cupboard and returned with a long rectangular box. Inside the box were ten different colored packets. Sophie carefully inspected the selection and then plucked a tiny magenta envelope. "*Oui*, raspberry I think. And for you?" she asked, opening the tea box in my direction.

The only kind of tea I drank was cold, had a big slice of lemon in it, and lots and lots of sugar. But when Sophie dropped the little baggy into her porcelain cup of steaming water and the rich, sweet scent of rosebuds and raspberries wafted through the air, I couldn't resist.

"If your Razzberry Pink's store sold perfume, this is what it should smell like!"

I agreed. Sophie was fascinated by the idea of a store devoted to pink.

"Raspberry please, *merci*," I said, trying to imitate Sophie's graceful steps—tearing open the tea sachet and lowering the bag into the water. The sugar cubes were in a bowl nearby, but the tea smelled so sweet already I decided to skip the sugar and took a sip. BIG MISTAKE! The hot tea burned my tongue and it definitely wasn't sweet.

Sophie didn't seem to notice my reaction as she lifted the cup with her wrist gracefully arched, her pinkie extended. She took a tiny sip and continued telling me about Philippe and Alain's big presentation in science class the week before. I couldn't help noticing how much Sophie sounded and looked like her mother as she spoke and daintily sipped her tea. I think Katani would call Madame Morel's look "classic" and Sophie's look "modern," but they both had a certain flair that made it clear they were mother and daughter. Sophie and Katani should definitely meet someday, I thought.

It was nearly 9:30 p.m. when we finished dinner.

"May I help with the dishes?" I asked.

"Oh, no, my dear Charlotte, *merci beaucoup*—thank you so much," Madame Morel said, glancing at the clock. "It's a school night for Sophie … you girls must get ready for bed. You have a busy week ahead of you, and you have had a very long day, Charlotte."

"Thank you for dinner, Madame Morel. It was delicious beyond belief," I said.

Madame grabbed my hands. "How you talk, Charlotte, so amusing. *Je t'en prie*, you're welcome, my dear Charlotte. A special celebration for a great friend," Madame Morel replied graciously.

"Before you leave the table, we must make a toast," Monsieur Morel announced.

Everyone raised their glasses.

"To Charlotte. *Bienvenue à Paris*," Monsieur Morel clinked his glass against mine.

"To Charlotte!" Sophie cheered.

"To Madame Morel—for an amazing dinner," I added.

"To old friends," Madame Morel smiled and raised her glass high.

We all sipped our drinks and sat in silence for a few moments, full of good food and the memories of a wonderful evening.

★

Sophie fell asleep right away that night. I, on the other hand, was still too wound up. Every cell in my body buzzed with excitement. Was it only this morning that I had been in my own bed all the way across the Atlantic? I knew I would never fall asleep if I continued tossing and turning, so I slipped out of my bed and tiptoed to Sophie's desk. I started up the computer as quietly as I could and connected to the Internet.

I checked the clock on the computer screen. 10:15 p.m. I counted back on my fingers. Nine fifteen. Eight fifteen. Seven fifteen. Six fifteen. Five fifteen. Four fifteen. No wonder I wasn't tired—it was only 4:15 in the afternoon! Half of me was in America and the other half in Paris. *Très bizarre*! I thought.

To: Katani, Maeve, Isabel, Avery
From: Charlotte
Subject: Hello from Paris!

Dear BSG,
I still can't believe it ... I'm
actually here, in PARIS! I'm at
Sophie's apartment right now. Her mom
made an amazing dinner to celebrate my
visit. I forgot how good real French
food tastes! The plane ride was fun.
There was a nice man sitting next to me
(Mr. Peckham) who I talked to, and that
helped the time pass quickly. He's from
England, but he's lived in Paris for
over fifty years! Just wanted to say
hello and tell you that *je suis arrivée
à Paris*! Miss you lots!

bisous,
Charlotte

I was still wide awake, so I decided to check *The Boston Globe* website to see what was happening back home.

Home, I thought. What a flip-flop! Just a short time ago I was wondering what was happening in Paris because I still considered it to be my home.

Same old news. There was trouble in the Middle East.

Would that ever change? I wondered. The front-page story was about a possible strike by public transportation workers. Blah, blah, blah, as Maeve would say. I was about to sign off, but I noticed the word "Picasso" under the Arts and Entertainment heading. I clicked on the story and scanned it quickly.

A Picasso sketch had been stolen from a Boston home. Odd, I thought … Isabel had been so excited that I would get to see Picasso's artwork in Paris, and the picture that had been taken was an original sketch from the neighboring community of Newton, not that far from where we lived in Brookline. The police had no leads on the thief, and the case was under investigation.

When I turned off the light on the desk and logged off the computer, it was just after 11 p.m. Paris time—5 o'clock at home. The computer desk was only five steps away from my roll-away bed, but as I crept back I somehow managed to trip over my suitcase. Thankfully, I caught myself on the edge of the bed, but cringed as my tiny flashlight rolled off the mattress and landed with a loud *kerplunk* on the hardwood floor. I peeked at Sophie, but she only squirmed and rolled over.

I picked up the flashlight and quietly climbed back into bed. As I began to drift off to sleep, I dreamed of Orangina wandering the streets of Paris. He wasn't slinking around on all fours. Instead he was wearing a tuxedo, walking down the street like a regular person, and talking to me in a French accent. "Oh, my dear Charlotte, it is *fantastique* to have you back in Paris. Won't you join me for a cup of tea? I want to tell you everything that's happened since you went away."

BREAKING NEWS!

PICASSO SKETCH STOLEN!

> ▶ Story
> "I can't believe someone would do this! I'm furious!!!"

A&E

CELEBRITY

✄ Friend or foe? They look like friends, but act like enemies ...

Is this a new friendship model or a recipe for disaster?

NEWS

LOCAL

More kids volunteering
Recent reports cite an upswing in ten to fifteen year olds volunteering in a variety of areas. "It is so exciting to hear that our youth is so committed to helping

📷 **Video Extra!**
Local kids clean up alley ...

~ V ~

Le Dernier Cri

THE LATEST FASHION

WHEN I WOKE UP, the room was bathed in a soft light. I blinked as I tried to adjust to my surroundings. This wasn't my bed. Where was Marty? Why wasn't he curled in a ball at the foot of the bed? Then it hit me ... I was in Paris.

Sophie had closed the curtains to let me sleep, but she left a small lamp on so I wouldn't be confused when I woke up. Her bed was empty. I looked at my watch. It said 9 o'clock. I felt wide awake, which was especially surprising since it was 3 o'clock in the morning back in Boston.

Yikes! Sophie must have left for school over an hour ago. And I was supposed to go to school with her! Sophie's parents both worked. Had they left me in the apartment alone?

I grabbed my robe and stumbled into the living room. Even though the Paris sky was as gray as the rooftops, the Morels' living room was filled with a soft, bright light. The light in Paris always made me feel like I was in a painting. It cast a glow that made everything seem more real and more magical at the same time. Maybe that's why there are so many great French painters, I thought. I paused at the window and gazed out. Between rooftops of buildings cluttered with stacks of clay chimney pots, I caught a glimpse of the silver waters of the River Seine.

"*Bonjour!*" Madame Morel called out cheerfully, stepping into the living room to join me.

"Good morning, Madame Morel," I replied. "I'm sorry I slept so late. I wish Sophie had woken me up for school!"

"Do not worry, *ma chérie*. We decided that after your long day of travel, you should sleep well so you will feel rested. I have the day off from work today, so I will bring you to school in the afternoon … that will be plenty of time for a visit."

For breakfast Madame laid out *omelette au fromage*, slices of *baguette* topped with strawberry jam, and a glass of freshly squeezed orange juice. I eagerly dug into the delicious cheese omelette and sipped the sweet juice.

After breakfast I got dressed, and while I was rummaging around in my bag, I realized that I hadn't packed my favorite brown shoes. I hit my head lightly with the heel of my hand. *Nice job, Char*, I thought. Since I had a week's worth of clothes to cram into one suitcase, I had repacked it several times to make it all fit. Even though I had my trusty checklist, I must have left my shoes on the floor back home at the last minute—*no wonder* everything had finally fit. I hoped I hadn't forgotten anything else. I didn't want to come across as completely unstylish. After all, I was in one of the world's most fashionable cities.

My sneakers would be fine for walking around Paris, but if the Morels took us out to a fancy dinner, well … I would stick out like a sore thumb. At least I didn't have to worry about that right away. For now, I put on a pair of corduroy pants and a light, warm sweater. The brown shoes would have looked better with the outfit, but I had no choice. I grabbed my ski jacket and went to the living room.

"You plan on exercising this morning before we go to the school?" Madame asked with a twinkle in her eye as she nodded toward my running shoes.

"I accidentally left my nice shoes back at home. I know the sneakers and ski jacket scream 'American,' but they're all I have."

"There's nothing wrong with your ensemble, Charlotte. If everyone looked the same, it would be terribly boring, *n'est-ce pas*—don't you think?"

I nodded.

Madame smiled and stepped back. "But I'm sure we can find some other shoes for you to wear if you would like. Hmmm," she said, looking at my feet. "Sophie wears a 37, and your feet look a little larger."

European sizes are different from American sizes, but just from seeing Sophie's shoe collection, I could tell that her feet were smaller.

"One moment," Madame held up a finger. She

retreated to her bedroom and shut the door. When Madame returned, she had a satisfied smile on her face. She had changed into tailored black pants, a cream-colored sweater, and black high-heels with pointy toes.

"Come," she said as she put on her gray wool coat and black scarf. "Bring your bag—we will do a few errands and then I will leave you at school. It is arranged."

Madame Morel loved to "arrange" things—it was her passion. I was anxious to know exactly what Sophie's mom had arranged for me, but I was too timid to ask.

I hurried to keep up with Madame Morel as she briskly clicked along the sidewalk to the *métro* station. After we had been walking for a few minutes, I got the weird feeling that I was being watched. When I looked over my shoulder, I saw a few people walking behind us. At first I thought my imagination was getting the better of me, but then a man in a black raincoat caught my attention. Almost immediately, he wheeled around and walked into a store. When I turned around again, I had to double my pace to catch up with Madame Morel. Her black heels made a sharp ringing sound on the metal steps as we descended into the station.

The *métro* wasn't overcrowded at midmorning like it was during rush hour. We found two seats together toward the back of the train. I tried not to stare at the people around me, but I couldn't help it. Sophie was right—it was easy to pick out the tourists by their cameras, maps, and casual clothing.

✦

We emerged from the *métro* station in front of la Samaritaine—one of the largest department stores in Paris—where Madame worked as a buyer in the baby clothing department.

"First … the shoes," she said with a knowing smile.

"Huh?" I asked as Madame took off in quick, determined strides toward the shoe department. I ran a few steps to catch up with her.

"You are on vacation, Charlotte. It is a time for special treats, like new shoes," Madame explained as she pulled two pairs of shoes off one of the racks.

I stopped counting the number of shoes I tried on over the next hour. Madame rejected this shoe as too sophisticated or that shoe because it would be *démodé*— out of fashion—by next year. She ruled out some shoes because they were not durable enough and others because they would show dirt or scuff marks. Finally she settled on three pairs for me to try on.

"Any of these will do. But you must choose the shoe that makes you feel confident and comfortable. Comfort is important, yes? But if your shoes make you feel confident, they will carry you through the world for the next year." I knew Katani would approve of Madame Morel's advice. She was always saying that true style was all about finding clothes that made you feel good about yourself.

I looked for the price tag.

"No, no! Do not worry about the price. They are all great quality. They are all worth every penny. These will be *un petit cadeau* … how do you say? … a gift from me, to celebrate your return to Paris. And do not protest, I only pay half with my discount."

I knew it was no use arguing with Madame Morel. She was a very generous—and very stubborn—lady. "Thank you so much, Madame Morel," I said. "This is so nice of you. I'll always think of you when I wear them."

I turned to the tough task of choosing a new pair of shoes. I loved the looks of all three. One pair I put aside because they were not as comfortable as the others. Switching off between the other two pairs, I practiced walking up and down the narrow strip of carpet several times, repeating in my head, "Confidence! Confidence! Confidence!" One pair had a higher, chunkier heel, and I wobbled a little bit during my model walk. So I decided to go with the soft, chestnut brown pair with a low block heel. The shoes were elegantly stitched with a simple flower design.

"Excellent choice," Madame remarked. "You will wear them now, no?"

"Of course!" I exclaimed, giddy with excitement. I shoved my sneakers in the bottom of my bag.

"Next … a coat," Madame declared, and then grabbed my arm and marched me off toward the coat department.

"A coat?" I asked bewilderedly. "But I already have a jacket. Really, I don't need a coat, thank you, Madame."

"Every young woman needs a proper dress coat. It will serve you for years, and with a good coat and the right

"*After all, I was in one of the world's most fashionable cities.*"
~ pg. 72

shoes, you will look *splendide* no matter what else you are wearing," Madame said as she summoned the saleswoman.

"But Madame, dress coats are very expensive! I can't accept another gift from you, it's—it's too much."

"*Ma chérie*, you must. There will be no argument. There is a sale on coats, and with my discount, it will not be so expensive."

I nodded slowly, not knowing what else to do. I was overwhelmed by Madame's generosity.

The saleswoman busily followed Madame's directions. Just as with the shoes, Madame Morel went about weeding out unacceptable coats. She sorted through the racks, making quick decisions *"Mauvaise couleur. Trop lourd. Quelle horreur!"* She was getting very excited and I had a hard time following her French.

"*Qualité, qualité, qualité*," Madame reminded me as I tried the coats on. "And when you can't afford the quality you desire, you must exude the quality yourself. Project it from deep inside you. No matter what you are wearing, the air of confidence is always the first thing you put on." I felt like Cinderella, with my very own fairy godmother creating my new wardrobe.

After trying on countless coats, I finally narrowed it down to two. I asked Madame which she liked better. She said she liked them both and that I must be the one to make the final decision.

"I don't know," I hesitated. "I always find it hard to keep up with fashion DOs and DON'Ts. My friend Katani is really into fashion … she helps me pick out clothes sometimes." I thought wistfully for a moment that it would be so nice if my mother was here picking out shoes with me and Madame Morel. But I let that moment pass. My dad told me, "It's important to live in the present, but cherish your memories."

"We will try this then. What colors bring out your complexion and the color of your eyes? This is better than depending on the whim of fashion. For you … always remember earth tones—the rich, dark reds, purples, and browns of the earth, the deep green of the forest, and the midnight blue of the night sky are best. Silver, not gold, accents your complexion."

I couldn't wait to write down Madame's fashion tips in my notebook. Katani would be *very* impressed.

"I think I'll take this purple coat because … well, because it matches the hat that my friend Katani made for me." I pulled out the purple beret from my bag. "And it's my favorite color," I added.

"Your friend made a beautiful choice for you. She has a good eye, no?"

"She wants to be a fashion designer. In fact, she asked me to take a few pictures of the latest Parisian fashions in the windows to give her an idea of what's new."

"I know just the street. But first, I will show you how to wear a hat. *Un chapeau* can pull together an outfit like no other accessory. It can soften and frame the face and give a young woman an extra boost of confidence. Your hair is a beautiful honey color, and a great length to accent your face. With the confidence this hat will bring, people will think to themselves *très chic* when you walk by."

Every time she said "confidence," I felt a little bit taller.

Madame went on. "A square face should wear a hat with a medium brim. An oval face can wear a large, straight, or floppy brim. Your face is between oval and round. For you, this beret is *parfait* … perfect!!" she said, gently pulling my shoulders back and then lifting my chin so my eyes met hers. "Lovely." Madame expertly dipped the hat slightly to the right side and pronounced me *"Magnifique."*

I looked in the mirror and had to admit I did look fabulous … and *très française*. I couldn't help smiling. Maybe it wasn't the air in Paris or the latest fashions that made Parisian women look *chic*. Maybe it was simply a skill passed down from mother to daughter.

I rolled my puffy ski coat into a tight little ball and shoved it into my messenger bag along with my wallet, notebook, and my surprise gift for my old classmates. It was a good thing I had left the Picasso book at the Morels' apartment—my bag was chock full as it was.

Madame and I went to the elevator, but instead of pushing "ground floor" she pressed the top floor button. I wondered if she had made a mistake. But when the elevator door opened, my heart jumped at the sight before me. We stepped through two large glass doors and onto the terrace of the department store. Below us, the city of Paris and all of its treasures stretched out in every direction. It was the perfect panoramic view of the city I had called home for two years—a city that still had an important place in my heart.

"One of the many advantages of working at La Samaritaine," Madame said, gesturing toward the view. "It is the best view in the city, *n'est-ce pas?*"

I had to catch my breath as my eyes drank in the vision before me ... the Arc de Triomphe, the Eiffel Tower, Napoleon's tomb, the Notre-Dame and the Sacré Coeur churches, and there—running through it all—the silver waters of the River Seine. I wanted to pinch myself to make sure it was real.

From La Samaritaine we took the *métro* to Avenue Victor Hugo and rue du Faubourg St-Honoré, where we walked past row after row of boutiques full of the latest creations of Yves Saint Laurent, Chanel, Lanvin, Balmain, Givenchy, Christian Dior, and other top French designers.

Madame led me to the windows she considered most appealing and I took pictures, careful not to use the flash to avoid the reflection off the windows. I hoped the pictures wouldn't come out too dark on this foggy day. I used up all but three of the pictures on Katani's camera, just in case I saw some other fashions later in the week.

Madame Morel stopped in one of the smaller boutiques and bought a silky scarf. "One more gift for you," she said as she handed it to me. My scarf had a brown, lavender, and white pattern. I bought a similar one for Katani with lots of yellow—her favorite color—in it. She would love it.

When we finished our shopping, Madame hurried me over to Collège St-Louis where I would spend the afternoon visiting my former classmates.

VI

La Rentrée

BACK TO SCHOOL

FOR A MOMENT I FELT like I was in a time warp … as if I were still a student at Collège St-Louis and would be punished for arriving late to class. The school day in Paris was longer than in the United States, lasting from eight in the morning until five in the afternoon, including a long break for lunch. French students had Wednesdays off, but they went to school for a half-day on Saturday. Despite the longer hours, I loved the schedule in France. We worked very hard in school, but there was built-in time to relax. Maybe I could propose the French school schedule to Mrs. Fields, the principal at Abigail Adams Junior High.

Madame explained that she was allowing Sophie to take Tuesday off and because there were teacher meetings on Thursday and Friday, Sophie would not have to return to school until Saturday morning—the day I was leaving. I couldn't believe it—we would have *four full days* to find Orangina and to explore our old haunts.

Madame stopped to check in at the office first, and then walked me to the third floor English class, leaving me at the door.

Sophie's eyes brightened when she spotted my new coat and shoes. She gave me a thumbs up and a big smile from across the room.

After spending half a day with Madame, I felt like a completely different person. I definitely felt more "confident," that word she kept repeating, and even less klutzy. Fashion had always seemed like a puzzle that I was too busy to figure out, but Madame had made it seem easy and fun. Both Katani and Madame gave the same advice ... true fashion isn't about wearing the trendiest clothes, but about figuring out who you are and what makes you happy inside... and letting that shine through.

The English teacher, Madame de Robein, welcomed me to her class and gestured to an empty seat.

"Hello, Charlotte," Philippe said as I sat down at the empty desk next to him. The French students used to love practicing their English on me.

I smiled. "*Bonjour*, Philippe. *Ça va*? How are you?" Although we hadn't kept in touch during the past months, Philippe and I had been pretty good friends when I lived in Paris. It was good to see him again. He was definitely cute, though in my opinion, not as cute as Nick Montoya back home. Nevertheless, I knew Maeve would approve.

"We will have a conversation in English," Madame de Robein announced. "Although Charlotte speaks French very well, I want you to ask questions in English and Charlotte to answer in English. This is a wonderful opportunity for you to practice your English-speaking skills. Charlotte, would you mind coming to the front of the room so the class can see you?"

I looked at Sophie. She shrugged. I had no idea I was going to be part of today's lesson … I was glad the class would only last about an hour. It made me nervous to be the center of attention. But I was flattered that Madame de Robein thought my French was good.

"Do you live in New York City?" a tall girl in the front row asked.

"No, I live near Boston, in Massachusetts."

"Have you ever been to New York?"

"Yes."

"Have you met Beyoncé?"

"No."

And so it went … about forty-five minutes of somewhat silly, but not too embarrassing questions. The only time I didn't know what to answer was when a girl asked a rude question about our president. I just glared.

"Charlotte has brought a treat for the class, Madame," Sophie spoke up, "May we serve it now?"

I was so wrapped up in answering all those questions, I'd almost forgotten about my special treat. I brought my messenger bag up to Madame's desk, unzipped it, and pulled out the ski jacket on top. Once free from the tight space of my bag, it puffed out, expanding as if it were alive. The right sleeve flopped across the desk, pushing a small tin toward the edge of the desk. I reached for the tin, but it plunged over the edge, hit the floor with a loud TWANG, bounced once, and rolled noisily down the center aisle. Sophie jumped to her feet and scrambled after it as the class giggled. Thankfully, the tin of pushpins didn't pop open … that would have been chaos.

I put the ski jacket on Madame's swivel chair and pulled a jar of peanut butter and a box of crackers from my messenger bag.

"Is anyone allergic to *cacahouètes* … peanuts?" I asked. I knew that peanut allergies could be really serious. No one raised their hand, so I spread a glob of peanut butter on each cracker and Sophie passed them out on paper napkins.

I explained how popular peanut butter was in the United States … it was almost unheard of in France.

A girl named Céleste made a face and held her nose. She murmured something in French to her best friend, Chantal. Céleste and Chantal were never nice to me when I was in their class. I called them the *Chuchoteurs*—the Whisperers. They were the French version of the Queens of Mean, Anna and Joline, the star mean girls at Abigail Adams. I have decided that the language of mean kids is universal—they whisper private jokes, point, and laugh really loudly at everything. They try to make everyone else feel left out, and most of the time, they succeed.

Madame pointedly cleared her throat. "Céleste, this is English class. If you have anything to say, you must say it

in English."

Two bright pink patches appeared on Céleste's cheeks, and she bit her lip.

"Don't mind her," Philippe whispered to me, his eyes holding mine for a brief second. "Céleste never has anything nice to say about anyone or anything."

I smiled gratefully at Philippe.

"Uglgh! Ischtuck to the top of my moughf!" a boy named Pierre struggled to speak through the peanut butter gooeyness.

"Don't be disgusting, Pierre, close your mouth when you chew," Chantal said haughtily.

Madame de Robein shot both students a warning look.

In the end, it seemed as if my peanut butter-and-cracker idea was an overall hit. Philippe and a girl named Aimée asked for seconds, so I made them little peanut butter and cracker sandwiches.

"OK, *mes amis*, time to pack up your things and go," announced Madame de Robein just before the hour was up. "*Merci beaucoup*, Charlotte, for all that you've shared. It was so nice to see you again."

"Thanks for having me," I said. "It's good to be back."

VII

Les Temps S'écoule Comme de L'eau

TIME IS LIKE A RIVER

I SMELLED THE SEINE before I saw it—an exotic blend of freshness and fishiness at once exhilarating and foul. Sophie and I walked from school toward the water to begin our search for Orangina. I rushed forward to the end of the street to catch a glimpse of the river I once called home. On this overcast, windless day, the river lay like a ribbon of silver threading its way under bridges and curving through the oldest part of Paris.

My breath caught in my chest when I saw our old houseboat. I wanted to run down the quay and jump aboard … but I knew it was not my home anymore. I wondered with a pang if Orangina, wherever he was, felt the same way.

Most people instantly picture the Eiffel Tower when they think of Paris. I think of the Seine. A little motorboat slowly putted by, and I could imagine how the houseboat would rock as the wake set it moving. The tin chandelier over the kitchen table would still be swinging five minutes after the boat was out of earshot. I could hear our neighbor Monsieur Duprée shouting in French about those *"stupides bateaux"* —stupid boats.

When we moved in to the houseboat, it was fully equipped with pots, pans, and china. I loved the country feel to the place—it was very rustic and lived-in and felt almost like camping in the middle of one of the most beautiful cities in the world. The kitchen stove usually needed to be coaxed to work ... the kitchen in Sophie's apartment was a modern marvel in comparison.

And then there was the mud—oh, the mud! There was always mud after the water rose and receded. No matter how often Dad and I wiped our feet, one of us always managed to track mud through the entire houseboat.

Parisian life revolves around the Seine and I love every bit of it: couples walking hand-in-hand along the cobblestone quay in the early evening, the rowing club passing by in the morning, even the bellowing squawk of the herons. There was always barge traffic from the sightseeing boats. Once I awoke to a tapping at my window and was surprised to look out and be face to face with a swan.

To me, the Seine was the essence of Paris. Orangina felt as connected to the river as I did. He loved watching birds flit from branch to branch on the trees that hung low over the water. And his favorite thing to do was prowl the banks for hours on end.

✤

"You see the quay right here under this bridge?" Sophie motioned, pointing. "This is where I saw Orangina, I promise. It was definitely him; there is no doubt in my mind. He turned when I called his name. For a moment I thought he would come to me, but I took only one tiny step forward and he scampered away. In a flash, he was gone. Just like that."

I couldn't help laughing at Sophie. Her hands were going a mile a minute, making little cat scampering motions. I looked at the place she had pointed to and suddenly felt a wave of disappointment. From the moment Sophie emailed me, I imagined coming to Paris and finding Orangina exactly where Sophie had spotted him. I'd expected him to jump in my arms.

"Charlotte, you look tired."

"I'm just worried, Sophie. I know it's kind of silly, but I wanted so much to find him right here waiting for us. Where should we look next?"

"Come, I know the way to revive your spirits," Sophie said with a smile.

I followed her across Pont Louis-Philippe down rue St-Louis-en-l'Ile. As I walked, I breathed in the moist smell of the river air. Overhead, I could see a "V" of geese in the gray sky above La Cathédrale de Notre Dame.

Through the bare branches of the trees, I could see every detail on the old buildings. Ile St-Louis was like a step back in time. I always felt that once I crossed the bridge, I'd slipped back to another century—maybe the 1600s or 1700s.

I almost expected to see a horse-drawn carriage clopping down the street. Instead, a moped sped past me and brought me abruptly back to the twenty-first century.

"I am sure you have been dreaming of this place, Charlotte," Sophie remarked. "I don't know how you survived this long without it."

Sophie didn't seem to notice the beautiful scene before her as she chattered and walked with a purpose. I knew just where she was headed. There it was just a block away—the green-and-white-striped canopy of Berthillon, the most famous—and yummiest!—ice cream parlor in the city.

In the summer, the line stretches down the street and around the corner. Even on this overcast day, there was still a line for the best sorbet and ice cream on the European continent. They have the most exotic flavors, ones I haven't yet found in Boston: blood-orange, prune, fig, and armaganac. I didn't have to look at the list. I knew exactly what I wanted ... chocolate hazelnut. *C'est délicieux!*

In Paris, like in most cities, there are lines for everything, but the French wait as elegantly as they do for everything else. They don't whine or complain if the lines are excruciatingly long ... they just accept it as a part of life and enjoy the moment of peace.

While Sophie and I waited, my messenger bag started to feel really heavy. I took it off and held it to my side, accidentally brushing against a passerby. *"Excusez moi,"* I said more than once, unable to stay out of the way in the growing crowd of people.

I filled Sophie in on my shopping expedition with her mother. "She was so generous, Sophie … I don't know how to thank her. I absolutely love my new coat, it's wicked nice!"

Sophie burst out laughing. "Wicked nice?" she mocked me gently. "That is your new American way of speaking, no?"

I blushed slightly and laughed. "I think I picked it up from Avery. It must be a Boston thing, though, because Isabel, who's from Detroit, always laughs when Avery says 'wicked,' too."

"You teach me so much, Charlotte! I am sure *Maman* enjoyed her time with you this morning. She loves to shop. She's always bringing home new things for me to try on. She has a good eye for color … that purple coat is perfect on you," Sophie added, touching the sleeve.

Suddenly, out of the corner of my eye, I saw the dark shape of a man in a blue-and-white striped raincoat and hat. He was waiting at the back of the line. I did a double take. Had I seen this man before? I couldn't see his whole face because he had turned in the other direction, but something about the shape of his shoulders, his size, seemed familiar. Of course, on a day like today, there were hundreds of older Parisian men wearing raincoats and hats. But there was something about the way he reached up and smoothed his mustache. The movement was so familiar. It couldn't be … or could it? Could it be Mr. Peckham? What were the odds that I would run into him

"There it was just a block away—the green-and-white-striped canopy of Berthillon, the most famous—and yummiest!—ice cream parlor in the city."   ~ pg. 91

again in a city of seven million? I put my bag on the ground for a second and craned my neck to try to get a better view, but the man seemed to have vanished into thin air. I turned back to Sophie and slung my bag over my shoulder one more time.

"There was a man back there that looked just like Mr. Peckham ... you know, the older man I told you about from the plane? He's gone now though ... one second he was there, and the next second he wasn't," I explained to Sophie, getting some euros out of my wallet as we inched closer to the front of the line.

"He must not love ice cream as much as we do," Sophie said.

★

It was getting chilly as the evening approached, so Sophie and I chose to sit inside by the window and people-watch as we ate our ice cream. All over the city, hundreds of Parisians were doing the same. Half the fun of being in Paris is to observe passers-by. The French love cafés and strolling arm in arm. They chatter furiously, using their hands as punctuation marks. Everyone looks like they just stepped out of a movie. It's almost like watching one, but better.

We slowly savored our ice cream ... my chocolate hazelnut and Sophie's fig. When I had scraped the last mouthful out of the paper cup, I reached for my messenger bag and found ... nothing.

"Sophie! My bag … it's gone!" I scrambled out of my seat, looking in all different directions.

Sophie jumped up as well. "Are you sure you brought it with you? Perhaps you left it at school. We can walk right back there and look for it."

"No. Yes. I mean no, I didn't leave it at school. I'm sure I brought it here with me. I remember I had it in line … I kept hitting people with it by mistake. Then when we sat down, I put it right here next to me. Near the door."

Sophie glanced around. "Perhaps someone accidentally picked it up. Let's go out to the sidewalk right away and look at the people nearby."

I looked out at the mixture of tourists and locals walking around and felt overwhelmed. There were a million different directions that someone carrying the bag could have gone. "I don't know, Soph … How could someone have thought the bag was theirs? It has that patch that Katani sewed on for me. No one else has the same bag. It's a Kgirl original … my favorite bag of all time. It's irreplaceable!" I could feel tears starting to well up.

"What was in it?" Sophie asked, sitting back down at the table.

"Everything," I said, checking to make sure my notebook and pen were still in my back pocket. "My ski jacket, my running shoes … um, the rest of the jar of peanut butter … the disposable camera that Katani gave me. I even took all these pictures for her this morning. My wallet. Thank goodness I left Chelsea's digital camera at home. And I took out the Picasso coloring book before we left this morning, too. Oh no! My passport was in there! How can I get back into the U.S. without my passport?"

"Try not to panic, Charlotte. I'm sure that people lose their passports all the time. We can ask my father what to do. Come, Charlotte. Let's leave your name and our telephone number with the people working at the counter. Perhaps whoever picked the bag up will bring it back."

Charlotte's Journal

I am <u>very</u> upset. I don't understand why someone would have taken my bag. It's not like I look rich or anything ... and how much money do kids usually even carry with them? I guess it could have happened by accident, but it seems weird ... there were no other tables between ours and the door. Why would someone think they had left their bag right in that exact spot? I guess I should be grateful that Chelsea's digital camera didn't get stolen. I would have been so embarrassed to tell her that her nice, expensive camera was GONE. I'm trying to put the whole thing in perspective ... my dad uses that phrase a lot. Sophie says we'll go back to Berthillon's tomorrow to check and see if someone found it. I'm keeping my fingers crossed, but I can't help being frustrated. My trip was going along so perfectly before ... why did this have to happen?

VIII

Le Petit Navire

LITTLE BOAT

"GIRLS, WE ARE GOING OUT to a little, charming dinner this evening," Madame Morel announced shortly after we arrived back at the apartment. We had just filled Madame in on the missing bag, and she was very sympathetic. She gave me a warm hug and *la bise*. "This is a terrible welcome back!" she declared sympathetically.

I shrugged. "It was all so wonderful up until now. What am I going to do about my passport?" I was almost in tears. "I need that! Security is so tight these days, they'll never let me back home again."

"Now don't worry, Charlotte. It will all work out, I promise. We'll go to the U.S. Embassy tomorrow and straighten it out. This happens all the time," Monsieur Morel reassured me.

"Where are we going for dinner, *Maman*?" Sophie changed the subject quickly. I saw her glance at me and knew she was trying to take my mind off things. But more

French food was the last thing on my mind.

"We will walk to Petit Navire," Madame said. "You girls should be ready to go in about twenty minutes."

I went into the bathroom to wash my face and brush my hair. I changed into a light purple sweater, put on my new shoes and buttoned up my dark purple coat, glancing in Sophie's full-length mirror. My new outfit was perfect for a night on the town. I felt so grown up and sophisticated in it. *I'd feel even better if I only had my bag*, I thought with a sigh.

Sophie had changed into black pants, pointy black shoes with low heels, and a light blue sweater. She buttoned up her long black coat, and then we linked arms and walked down the hall to the living room. She always looked so stylish. It must be genetic, I thought—this ability to accessorize so cleverly.

"You girls look *très belles*," Monsieur Morel said. "Let me take a picture of you."

Sophie and I stepped in front of the fireplace and smiled for the camera, and then the four of us walked out the door and down the long staircase to the street.

★

I have never been so stuffed in my entire life. We started our meal with scruptillious (that's my word for amazingly scrumptious) *escargots à la bourguignonne*— snails stuffed with a buttery mixture of mushrooms and parsley. I had to close my eyes, though ... they tasted awesome, but they were slimy-looking things. After the appetizer, Madame encouraged us all to order soup. I had *la soupe aux oignions*. It was amazing—an onion soup that was salty, cheesy, and comforting all at the same time. I am going to put this on my list of French food to make for the BSG, I thought.

For my entrée, I chose *les moules au diable* … mussels in a spicy sauce. Of course, Monsieur Morel insisted upon the cheese course. After sampling *Brie*, Münster, *Tome de Savoie*, and *Cantal*, we took our time deciding on dessert. I ordered the Charlotte *russe* cake (no, it wasn't named after me, but I wish it were!) with pudding.

All throughout the delicious dinner, I kept forgetting and then remembering again the upsetting events of the day. At first, I was disappointed about not finding Orangina where I pictured her. Who would have thought it could get much worse? I just couldn't believe that someone would think my bag was theirs … it was one of a kind. Would I ever see my things again? And how would I get home?

When we got back to the Morels' apartment, Sophie and I went to her room to check our email and plan what we would do the next day.

While Sophie was on the computer, I wrote down all the things Madame Morel had taught me about fashion that day in my notebook. I was still freaked out about losing my bag, and writing about something else calmed me down a bit. I decided not to tell Dad about the missing bag quite yet. Sophie tried to convince me that it might be returned, but I knew the chances were slim. Even if a nice

"Most people instantly picture the Eiffel Tower when they think of Paris. I think of the Seine."

~ pg. 88

person took it by mistake, there was nothing inside the bag that would connect me to the Morels.

Sophie opened a bunch of emails from her classmates. Philippe had come up with the idea that they should have a party for me before I went back home to the States.

"How about Pizza Pino on Friday night? *Très américain, n'est-pas*?" Sophie asked. "It's a very popular place for our class to go."

It sounded like a great idea to me. I really wanted the chance to catch up with everybody. How fun!

"And we will be able to celebrate our wonderful week together in Paris—and hopefully the return of Orangina— before you must say *au revoir*," Sophie decided before emailing everyone that Friday night would be perfect.

"Did you notice the way Philippe was looking at you today?" Sophie asked as we got ready for bed and turned the lights out.

"No way!" I said, my cheeks feeling warm.

"Can you blame him? You looked *très chouette* in your new coat and shoes. And the hat was *magnifique*!"

"I have your mother to thank for that."

"Yes, she has what you call the eye, does she not?" Sophie commented.

"You do too, Sophie," I reassured my friend.

At that moment, I felt that familiar pang of sadness, realizing that I'd never gone and would never go on special shopping trips with my own mother. But I knew I was lucky to have someone like Mrs. Morel in my life. All mothers have their own special tips and advice to offer, and my morning with Sophie's mom had been a lot of fun. *Then again, I'm not just here to have fun*, I reminded myself. *I'm supposed to be looking for Orangina.*

"I've been here over twenty-four hours and I've barely even begun to search for Orangina," I told Sophie remorsefully. "I feel like I've let him down already."

"We will start tomorrow. You needed a day to get used to the city again. Don't worry, Charlotte ... we will find Orangina. That cat belongs with you. *Bonne nuit*," Sophie said. Moments later, her breath grew slower, more rhythmic, and I knew she was asleep.

```
To: Avery, Katani, Maeve, Isabel
From: Charlotte
Subject: English Class

Bonjour mes amies!
I visited my old school today—the English
teacher made me answer questions so the
students could practice their English
conversation. They think we all live in
NYC and know movie stars. I brought some
peanut butter for them to try ... they
thought it was weird to eat, but some
of them liked it ... except the
Chuchoteurs, of course. My Paris friends
are planning a pizza party for me on
```

Friday. A year ago I was just a regular
kid, and now I'm an American celebrity.
LOL! Still no sign of Orangina, but we
haven't spent much time looking for him
yet. Tomorrow we'll have all day.
Keep your fingers crossed.
Miss all of u!

Gros, gros bisous—Big, big kisses,
Charlotte

To: Dad
From: Charlotte
Subject: Miss You

Dear Dad,
Things are going well here ... it's
so much fun to be back in Paris!
Thanks again for letting me come here ...
I promise I'm being careful. The Morels
really liked the gift basket from
Montoya's. We haven't found Orangina
yet, but I hope, hope, hope we have
better luck tomorrow. Give Marty a
paw-five for me.

Love,
Charlotte

✤

I purposely didn't mention the coat or shoes to the BSG or Dad, and I definitely didn't mention the lost bag. I wanted to surprise everyone with my new look when I got back, and I figured there was no use worrying Dad with the missing passport and wallet until it was absolutely necessary.

I crawled into bed, covered myself with the big, pouffy comforter, but I still couldn't get to sleep. I tossed and turned. A half hour later, I was still wide awake, staring out the window as the moon rose over the rooftops. Just as the ocean tides are affected by the pull of the moon, I felt torn between Boston and Paris. I wanted to know what was going on back home, but at the same time I also wanted to stay in Paris longer. I checked my watch. It was almost midnight here, but dinner time back in Boston.

I couldn't help myself. I slipped out of bed to see if any of the BSG had checked their email yet.

To: Charlotte
From: Avery
Subject: SSDD (Same Stuff Different Day)

walked Marty today ... he says "woof!"
going back again tomorrow after school.
it's weird that kids in Paris don't
like peanut butter ... that stuff
ROCKS! What DO they like over there?

later,
Avery

To: Charlotte
From: Katani
Subject: school

hey girl!
how's paris?
too much homework here!
don't worry, the BSG will help u catch
up. seen any new fashion trends?
Say hi to Sophie for me ... tell her to
come visit!

miss u lots!
Katani

~ IX ~

Pas à Pas

STEP BY STEP

THE NEXT MORNING, I was groggy from my lack of sleep, but the bright sunshine helped me get out of bed. Even though it was sunny, I crossed my fingers that it was still cold enough outside to wear my new coat and my Kgirl hat again. I walked over to the window, pushed it open wide, and shivered. The temperature was cool … perfect weather for wearing a coat and a hat.

I heard someone moving around in the kitchen so I threw on my clothes and tiptoed out the door, careful not to wake up Sophie. The night before, Monsieur Morel said that he would bring me to the U.S. Embassy first thing in the morning.

"*Bonjour* Charlotte. Help yourself to some breakfast, and then we'll head to the Embassy. We'll get this straightened out right away," Monsieur Morel assured me. He was a very comforting kind of dad. I had a sudden pang of missing Dad. I wondered if he was at the computer writing—little Marty sitting comfortably on his lap.

I quickly drank a mug of hot chocolate and gobbled up a croissant, and soon we were out the door.

Thankfully, Monsieur Morel was able to act as my witness at the U.S. Embassy. He declared to the official that I was, in fact, Charlotte Elizabeth Ramsey, and not some crazy girl trying to bamboozle my way into getting a fake passport. The French official was acting very suspicious, but that was his job, after all. Luckily, my father had thought to fax Monsieur Morel a copy of my birth certificate just in case of an emergency.

It took quite awhile to get my new passport photo taken, but we finally made our way back to the Fifth Arrondissement, with my brand new passport safely stowed in the bag I borrowed from Sophie.

"Thanks so much for helping me, Monsieur Morel," I said when we were in the elevator of the apartment building. "I feel so much better know."

"You're very welcome, Charlotte." Monsieur Morel then opened up his wallet. "Here," he handed me some euro bills. "You'll need spending money for the rest of the week."

He was right—I would need the money. I had no choice but to accept the bills. "That's so nice of you, thank you, Monsieur Morel. I'll pay you back as soon as I get home."

"*Ce n'est pas nécessaire*, Charlotte," he replied. "It's not necessary—your father would do the very same for my little Sophie."

I smiled gratefully. When we walked through the

door, Sophie was in the hallway getting her things together for our day in the city.

"Any luck with the passport?" she asked.

I gave her a thumbs-up.

"*Génial!*" Sophie exclaimed. "Let's get going, then."

Sophie and I decided the night before that we should start our search for Orangina along the river. After all, it was Orangina's favorite place to hang around, with the many scraps of tasty fish. We planned to start and end our search at the houseboat—it had been home to Orangina for almost two years. He was bound to wander back there at some point.

We began our walk along the riverside just as the booksellers were setting up for the day.

Huge, dark green wooden boxes artistically lined the quay. Every morning *les bouquinistes* arrived to open their boxes and set out their secondhand books. Each stand was a jumble of everything you could possibly imagine, but it was beautiful in its own way. Dad and I used to love sifting through the stacks of secondhand books, maps, postcards, and old magazines to find treasures. Today, however, Sophie and I had more important things to do. I searched behind the dark green stalls, while Sophie showed the vendors my picture of Orangina. Most vendors took a peek at the picture, but no one had any recollection of seeing him. It seemed like everyone was too wrapped up in selling their goods to help us any further.

Sophie and I decided to cross over to l'Ile de la Cité via

"I used to think of the two islands—l'Ile de la Cité and l'Ile St-Louis—as two huge ships cruising through the heart of Paris." ~ pg. 111

le Pont-Neuf, a beautiful white stone bridge with twelve arches. When the sun shines, le Pont-Neuf glows, shimmering above the gray water. I could see the massive walls of Notre-Dame rising up behind the black branches of leafless trees. The walls gleamed like gold in the morning sun. I made a telescope with my hands to see if I could make out the famous gargoyles and flying buttresses.

Sophie and I paused on the bridge, scanning the banks for a glimpse of orange fur. Instead, my eyes were drawn to a figure in a khaki raincoat on the other side of the river. He had been walking at our pace, but as soon as we stopped, he stopped too. When he noticed that I had seen him, he took a stutter-step before he continued on, as if he wanted to hide.

"*Regardez*! Look!" Sophie cried.

My heart almost skipped a beat. Thinking Sophie had spotted Orangina, I turned to look where she pointed, but saw nothing out of the ordinary.

"Sorry. I saw a flash of orange, but it's only that little girl's jacket."

I shrugged. "It's OK ... we can't expect to find him right away. Did you see—"

"*Qu'est-ce que j'ai vu*? Did I see what?" Sophie asked.

When I looked back to point out the man in the khaki raincoat, he was gone. I scanned all the people walking along the quay, but the man had completely disappeared. I just couldn't even imagine that the man following us was Mr. Peckham. He was just too nice.

I shook my head, confused, and mumbled, "Never mind." The mysterious man I'd seen was wearing a different colored raincoat every time … what was that all about? Maybe I was just seeing things. Maybe with the time change my imagination was going wild. There didn't seem to be any other explanation for my strange sightings.

I used to think of the two islands—l'Ile de la Cité and l'Ile St-Louis—as two huge ships cruising through the heart of Paris. L'Ile de la Cité is studded with monuments and important buildings, the largest of all being la Cathédrale Notre-Dame. We crossed the windswept Paris plaza and stopped in front of the cathedral at a worn bronze plate set in the pavement. I was standing on le Point Zéro—the famous marker on the cobblestone from which all distances in France are measured.

In front of me, the massive walls of Notre-Dame stretched into the clear morning sky. I stared up at the huge rose window above the entrance. Though I'd seen it a hundred times before, I was still overwhelmed by its grandeur. I turned my attention to the gargoyles—scary, monster-like stone creatures near the top of the cathedral. Some people claim that the gargoyles were made to keep away evil spirits, but they're actually used to drain water from the cathedral's roof. I'd rather think that they were guarding Paris from evil.

Sophie looked at me and raised her eyebrows.

"Ready?" she asked. I nodded and inhaled a big breath of air. Climbing Notre-Dame was a ritual of ours. We used to climb it at the beginning of every season.

"Perhaps we will see Orangina from the top," Sophie laughed as we started up the narrow tower stairs.

"We should have brought binoculars," I said, wishing I had thought of that earlier.

It was 255 steps to the first level. When we were halfway up, the bells began to chime. The biggest ones sent out loud tones that I could feel echoing in the middle of my chest.

Huffing and puffing, we climbed 125 more steps to the top of the south tower. There we came face-to-face with the famous gargoyles. Their crazy eyes and snarly teeth gave me the shivers.

Sophie turned away. "Charlotte, look." She threw up her hands. From high above, we had a spectacular view of l'Ile de la Cité and the Seine. All of Paris was before us.

"Maeve would fall in love with this view," I told Sophie. "She'd be striking poses and begging me to take her picture."

"Maeve is the red-haired one, *non*? The one who loves to sing and dance?"

I nodded. "She's as glamorous as a movie star. She knows the dialogue of almost every movie she's ever seen by heart. I need to find the perfect Paris gift for her."

"Oh, for Maeve, your romantic friend, finding the perfect *souvenir* should not be too hard. After all, this is

"I turned my attention to the gargoyles—scary, monster-like creatures near the top of Notre-Dame."

~ pg. 111

the City of Love."

"Oh yes, Maeve will be easy. Avery is another story."

"Avery is the little one? *Non*?"

"Yes. She loves sports—anything and everything that has to do with sports. She's a great soccer player. She never seems to get tired, no matter how long she's been running and jumping all over the place. If Avery were here, she'd want to swing from the ropes of the church bells just like Quasimodo in *The Hunchback of Notre Dame*. She definitely wouldn't like anything cutesy or touristy … she's going to be very tricky."

"Hmm. I see. That will require some thought. I will think about it," Sophie promised.

From the high tower, we scanned the far edges of the island. There would be no way we could see Orangina from so far up, even if he was nearby. I did spot one cat not too far from the base of the cathedral, but it was a gray tabby … not the bright electric orange that made Orangina famous.

After our visit to Notre-Dame, we wandered through le Marché aux Fleurs—the flower market. Everyone in Paris went there to buy the freshest, most colorful flowers. I looked under daisies and behind huge pots of irises hoping to see Orangina's familiar face peering out at me. Instead, I was greeted with wonderful smells and bright blossoms. Where was that cat? I had the strangest feeling he was lurking somewhere close by.

From le Marché aux Fleurs we wound through the streets of l'Ile de la Cité. We saw plenty of cats, but no

Orangina. I got excited once when I spied what I thought was the tip of his tail. Orangina always walked holding his tail as straight and stiff as a flagpole. I saw this scraggly "thing" bobbing down a stone staircase. I ran to the base of the stairs and immediately felt foolish. What I'd thought was a cat tail was actually a *baguette* sticking out of a woman's shopping bag. I burst out laughing.

"What's so funny, *mon amie*?" Sophie asked.

When I shared my case of mistaken cat identity with Sophie, she started laughing and couldn't stop.

The woman with the *baguette* looked at us like we had lost our minds and marched off down the street.

By noon, we were ready for a break. We munched on *croque-monsieurs*, grilled ham and cheese—my favorite, and sipped on lemonade at Taverne Henry IV, a little bistro that was famous for its cheeses. It was one of Monsieur Morel's favorites, and the owner was one of his good friends. They both liked to talk cheese. Sophie said it got kind of boring after awhile.

After we refueled from our lunch break, we continued to the tip of l'Ile de la Cité. The far end of the island felt slightly removed from the rest of Paris. Traffic noise grew dimmer, and soon I could hear everything. The birds chirped in the trees and bocce balls tapped as older men, bundled up against the breeze, played their games under the low branches.

Sophie and I moved toward the fragile-looking spire of la Sainte-Chapelle. Once inside, the hushed interior of the cathedral soothed my jangled nerves. In the lower level, built for the servants, there were no fancy stained-glass windows, but the ceiling was painted with stars. I sat quietly and collected my thoughts as I gazed up at the stars. When I first moved to Brookline, I had thought that stars and books would be my only friends in my new home. That was before I met the BSG. Gently, Sophie touched my knee and motioned that we should go. I smiled up at her, grateful that I now had good friends on both sides of the Atlantic Ocean.

I couldn't leave la Sainte-Chapelle without going up the spiral staircase to peek into the upper chapel. We were surrounded by brilliant blues and vivid reds from the light that poured in through the stained-glass windows. Sophie and I spun around quietly with our arms outstretched, letting the colors whiz by us. I felt like I was at a fairy-tale ball.

After leaving la Sainte-Chapelle, we spent an hour exploring the shoreline. We walked along the island edge calling Orangina's name. I hoped with all my might that he would appear beneath a low tree branch or pop out from behind a garbage can. We wound our way back through the streets of l'Ile de la Cité and across the bridge. The quay, which had been rather quiet this morning, was now full of fishermen, artists, fortune tellers, and tourists. An endless stream of people moved down the sidewalk, as if in a colorful march. We had been smart to talk to the booksellers earlier this morning before they were too busy bargaining with customers to pay attention to us.

Sophie and I walked in silence, searching, always searching, for the hint of a tail or a paw or a flash of orange fur. It was beginning to feel like we were looking for a needle in a haystack.

We stopped for a minute in front of my old houseboat. It suddenly occurred to me that maybe Orangina had adopted another family along the Seine. I tried peering in windows of other houseboats as we passed by. I was both happy and sad when I didn't find his mysterious face looking back at me. I wanted Orangina to be safe, but I'd be jealous if he'd found a new home and a new family.

Sophie and I gave up our search for the day and walked dejectedly back down the quay. The late afternoon sun was still bright as we left the river. The Eiffel Tower stuck out above the skyline, looking majestic against the blue sky. The moon would be full tonight. Seeing couples walk hand-in-hand made me think of what Sophie had said about Philippe. I blushed. Philippe was like Nick in a way—very sweet and not immature (like some boys my age). Philippe was cute, but we really were just friends. It was funny that Sophie thought he liked me. I shook the thought away. I didn't want to think of Philippe right now. I wanted to find my lost cat!

After an entire day of looking for Orangina, all I had to show for it were blisters on my heels from my new shoes. On top of that, there was still no sign of my missing messenger bag. I must have looked pretty glum because

Sophie linked arms with me and started skipping. I had no choice but to run or skip to keep up with her.

"Sophie! You know I'm terrible at skipping. And we're not six years old. Why do you always make me do this?" I couldn't help giggling as I tripped my way down the path.

"That's why, Charlotte. To see a smile on your face again." Sophie stopped skipping abruptly and held on tight to my arm so I didn't topple to the ground. "I have an idea. Let's visit the Ménagerie. We have two hours before *Maman* will be expecting us for dinner. And it is so close to home."

"Oh yeah! Great idea, Soph. I love that place. It's just what we need." The Ménagerie is a little zoo in the Jardin des Plantes. It's really small compared to other zoos, but that's what makes it special. I wondered if Orangina ever visited the zoo.

"Come," Sophie grabbed my arm. "Let's walk back across le Pont-Neuf to the Menagerie. We can keep our, how do you say it, *our eyes peeled* for any sign of Orangina."

Even though it was late in the day, the zoo was still full of people of all ages. Sophie and I walked through the exhibits, spending the most time at our favorite—the African monkeys. They were so cute and curious. Some of them were very naughty and liked to throw fruit peels at the visitors. I guess it must be pretty weird to have people staring at you all day. I decided I would just smile and wave and walk quickly by their cage. With Chelsea's digital camera, I snapped a couple of pictures of Sophie as she posed near a funny-looking orangutan. I took a few pictures of the birds of prey for Isabel … she's always looking for inspiration for her next bird cartoon.

Sophie looked at her watch. "We must go now, Charlotte. It's almost time for dinner."

As we walked out of the Jardin des Plantes, I hoped tomorrow would be the day that I'd cuddle Orangina in my arms again.

```
To: Charlotte
From: Maeve
Subject: re: English Class

Hi Char!
It's so weird here without you! Kids at
school keep asking
where you are. Don't let the Whisperers
get you down.
BTW, Anna is sooo jealous that you are
in Paris. (Nothing's changed.) Any
cute boys around? Don't forget about us
while you're gone!

LOVE AND HUGS,
Maeve
```

~ X ~

Jour Pluvieux

RAINY DAY

ON WEDNESDAY MORNING I awoke to the sound of Sophie breathing deeply, clearly sound asleep. I looked at my watch—8:30 a.m. Late enough that she wouldn't be too mad at me for waking her up. I shook her shoulder lightly. "Sophie? Sophie," I whispered, not wanting to startle her.

"Uhhh," Sophie mumbled, rolling over.

"Sorry. I think we should get up now … we don't want to waste any time today. Orangina's out there somewhere, and we just have to find him."

"OK," Sophie answered, yawning and stretching before hopping out of bed.

Sophie and I quickly dressed in jeans and hoodies. Madame asked us to run down to the *épicerie* to buy fresh eggs for our breakfast crepes. It was drizzling when we left, but by the time we headed back with the eggs, it was beginning to come down hard. We laughed as we hurried along the street trying to dodge raindrops. We dashed inside Sophie's building, pausing to catch our breath. Sophie looked down and gasped, pointing to a spot behind my feet.

"Charlotte! *Voilà*. It's your bag!"

It *was* my bag. "I can't believe it! Where did this come from?" I asked, lifting the purple messenger bag high above my head and dancing around the foyer.

"Was it here when we left for the *épicerie*?"

"No. Definitely not."

"Well, maybe it was … we left quickly. Perhaps we just didn't notice," Sophie said with a shrug.

I stuck my head out the door and looked in each direction. There was no one in sight. "The bag is wet," I said. "Whoever put it here was outside in the rain."

"It's been raining for a while, though," Sophie noted.

"This is *incroyable*!" I cried. "But who? How could anyone have known where to return the bag? There was absolutely nothing in it that would have led them here." Completely baffled, I looked at Sophie.

Sophie couldn't come up with an explanation either. "*Je ne sais pas*, Charlotte," she shook her head helplessly. "I don't know … it seems like a miracle."

I slung the bag over my shoulder and quickly headed upstairs to the apartment. We dropped off the eggs in the kitchen and did a dance of joy with Madame Morel. Once we were inside Sophie's bedroom, I unzipped the bag and pawed through the contents.

"Is anything missing?" Sophie asked.

"Let's see ... here's my passport, and my wallet is right on top!" I opened up the wallet and counted my money—everything was as I had left it. Nothing had been stolen. "And here's my ski jacket, my running shoes, the jar of peanut butter, the box of crackers ... where's the camera? Oh wait! Here it is!" I held up the disposable camera. "Oh well, I might as well take the last few pictures and get them all developed today. I'm curious to see how the fashion photos came out. Say cheese ..." I said, pointing the camera at Sophie.

"Why *fromage*?" Sophie asked.

"Not *fromage* ... cheese! It's what Americans say instead of 'smile for the camera,'" I told her.

"Oh, I understand. Saying 'cheese' makes you smile. Cheese always makes me smile ... all I have to do is think of it. In France, we say, *ouistiti* ... remember?" Sophie asked.

"No. What is *ouistiti* again?" I asked. I had forgotten.

"A very small monkey from South America," Sophie explained. "Different word. Same result. Watch me. *Ouistiti*," she said, giving me a great "cheesy" smile.

I pushed the button down on the top of the camera but nothing happened. I checked the little window on top of the camera and realized that there weren't any pictures left. "Oh no," I told Sophie. "I thought there were a few left. At least I have Chelsea's digital so I can take pictures at the pizza party." I stuck the camera back into the messenger bag.

After we ate the crepes Madame Morel prepared,

Sophie and I went back to her room to get ready for another day of Orangina-searching.

"Sophie, this has been the strangest morning of my life. I just don't get it. There's *no way* anyone could have known where to find me. I guess I should just be happy to have my bag back, and that nothing's missing. But still … why did it disappear in the first place? And why is everything still in it? This is a complete mystery."

"Maybe it's a sign that we're going to have *bonne chance aujourd'hui*," Sophie suggested.

"Here's to today's good luck!" I crossed my fingers and Sophie did the same. "Let's go."

The rain had now slowed to a drizzle. Our first stop that morning was a one-day photo lab. We'd pick up the pictures at the end of the day. With any luck, we'd have Orangina with us.

The next stop was the houseboat—our very own Point Zéro of the search for Orangina. As we walked along the quay, many of the booksellers from the day before shook their heads as we passed to let us know they still hadn't seen the missing orange cat.

We slowly made our way down to the very tip of l'Ile St-Louis to le Pont des Arts. There are dozens of bridges that cross la Seine, but le Pont des Arts is my favorite. It is a wood-planked, cast-iron pedestrian bridge. It even has benches so people can sit on the bridge and soak up the beautiful surroundings. During the summer, Dad and I would sometimes eat a picnic supper on the bridge and watch the river at sunset. There's always a spectacular view, especially when the setting sun reflects off the gold dome of the Institute de France along the left bank of the river. We weren't often the only ones enjoying the sunset. Other picnickers, fancier than us, unpacked linen napkins, crystal glasses, and bottles of champagne. Maeve would be out of her mind here. She would insist that we have a fancy party in the park, dress up outrageously, and dance around. I wonder if Parisians would know what to do with Maeve?

As Sophie and I walked across the bridge, I could see the Louvre on the other side of the river. It was early and the plaza in front of one the largest art museums in the world was empty at this hour. Isabel would be so excited if she were first in line when the museum opened! There were so many things about Paris that I wanted to share with the BSG ... not just with pictures, but in person. As Sophie and I headed away from the Louvre into the narrow streets of the corner of Paris known as the Marias, or the Marsh, I thought about how cool it would be to show the BSG all around Paris someday.

The Marias was the district for serious shoppers. Katani would be in heaven. There were lots of antique stores, as well as toy stores, museum shops, fashion boutiques, and decorator shops. The streets were empty at the moment, and I was too focused on searching for Orangina to spend much time looking in shop windows. My eyes scanned each doorway, each alleyway, searching any possible hiding place for a glimpse of orange.

Occasionally, I'd look up, shading my eyes from raindrops. I didn't want to leave any area unsearched. Suddenly, I saw a cat in an apartment window above. It was orange!

"Sophie, look!" I said, pointing up at the window. But immediately, I realized that the cat's orange fur was way too light to be Orangina's. Orangina looked like an orange ball of fire … this cat looked like a creamsicle.

"No, never mind. That's not him. I should have known better. Orangina would never be cooped up inside like that … this is his prime time for roaming the streets."

We were on rue St. Paul when suddenly the sky opened up and large pellets of raindrops began spattering the narrow street. Sophie and I ducked inside a doorway to escape the downpour. I was thankful that Paris was a great city for doorways.

"There's no use looking for Orangina in this weather," I said to Sophie. "Cats hate to get wet … and Orangina *especially* hated it. Sometimes when it rained like this he would disappear for days."

"Look where we are!" Sophie pointed at a sign with a mechanical quill that slowly wrote the word "*Entrez*" over and over again. The letters would completely disappear and then the quill would write the word again. It looked like something out of a movie. The sign was hanging above a stairway that descended into Le Musée de la Curiosité et de la Magie—The Magic Museum. We took a school field trip there last year, and ever since, it's been one of my favorite haunts in Paris.

✤

"Let's go in while we wait for the rain to slow down," Sophie suggested.

Dodging the big puddles, we made our way to the magnificent red doors of the museum, which was housed in the basement of a huge stone mansion. The red carpet and well-lit stone walls inside kept it from feeling too dark and scary ... but it was just weird enough to make it cool. The Magic Museum had an amazing collection of all the magical stuff you could ever dream of! There were all sorts of stage props. I liked the boxes used for sawing people in half and the ones with false bottoms to make people "disappear." Sophie loved the distorted mirrors and trick portraits.

We watched a short magic show in the museum theater. Afterwards, I decided to splurge on a new magic wand in the gift shop. I still had a lot to learn, but I was actually a pretty good magician. My friends and I even had a magic act in the school talent show earlier this year.

Over falafel sandwiches at Chez Marianne's, I told Sophie all about the Abigail Adams Junior High Talent Show and how instead of a traditional rabbit, Avery had pulled Marty out of a hat!

Sophie giggled. "I can't wait to meet all of your Beacon Street Girls someday."

★

"We might as well find something else to do inside until the rain stops," Sophie said after lunch. It wasn't as bad as it had been earlier, but there was still a steady drizzle.

"I promised Isabel I'd visit the Picasso Museum. It's in this area, isn't it?"

"*Oui*, not too far away," she pointed in the right direction. We walked through the rain, linking arms under the umbrella Sophie had brought. I scanned the streets right and left, hoping to spot Orangina curled up in a doorway or hiding beneath a downspout. I was beginning to think that Orangina didn't want to be rescued.

When we arrived at the museum the sky opened up again, drenching us to the bone before we could make it indoors. Whatever happened to the City of Light?

The Picasso Museum was located in the "heart of historic Paris" in an old building—an old hotel, really. The brochure said the hotel was built in 1656 for a general named General Aubert de Fontenay. I guess he wanted all his friends to be able to stay with him. The museum had over 203 paintings, 191 sculptures, 85 ceramics, and over 3,000 other works of art. Some of them were really weird looking, like people with split faces made out of cubes. Sophie thought it was amazing that Picasso created so many drawings and paintings in his life.

It was interesting going up the stairs to the second floor and looking at the sprawling black-and-white tiled foyer below. It actually made my head spin for a minute. We saw the works from Picasso's Rose Period and Blue Period. My

"Some of them were really weird looking, like people with split faces made out of cubes." ~ pg. 127

favorite section, though, was a special exhibition on Picasso's circus paintings.

"Oh, Isabel would love this place," I told Sophie. "I'll have to find her a *souvenir* in the gift shop."

"Is she the fashion designer?" Sophie asked as we wandered through the museum shop.

"No, the artist," I told her. "Isabel is really talented. You should see her room. She makes *papier-mâché* birds, and some of them are hanging from her bedroom ceiling … they're beautiful! She also draws cartoons for the school newspaper."

In no time at all, I found the perfect gift for Isabel. It was a calendar and each month featured a different Picasso painting. She would love it. Before heading to the cash register, another calendar caught my eye—"Parisian Movie Favorites." I flipped through it and smiled … it was *so* Maeve. I loved finding the perfect presents. I liked to give my friends things that showed how well I knew them. It made the present really meaningful, and the giving part more fun.

When we left the Picasso Museum, we headed back toward the river.

"Wait, let's stop here," Sophie called after we'd walked for a little while. She pointed to a fancy jewelry shop with diamond, pearl, gold, silver, and platinum jewelry glittering in the windows.

"Why do you want to go there?" I asked in amusement. "There's no way either of us can afford this fancy bling.

Even the tiniest little thing must cost hundreds of euros. I think we should window shop."

"Bling," Sophie laughed. "You are so American now!" She squeezed my hand. "We're not going to buy anything today, Charlotte. But what if we were ever to suddenly become *riche* and *célèbre*? We must be prepared to be rich and famous." Sophie grinned.

Without another word, Sophie marched confidently into the store and I followed behind.

"*Bonjour, monsieur,*" Sophie said smoothly to the man behind the counter. "I would like to try on that pearl bracelet, please."

The man looked sternly at Sophie but unlocked the counter and pulled out the bracelet she pointed to. He unhooked the delicate clasp and re-attached it around Sophie's wrist.

"Oh, it's just perfect. Isn't it? It will look *génial* with my new black gown!" Sophie exclaimed.

"Uh … yeah. It's beautiful" I tried unsuccessfully to smother a laugh.

"May I help you, miss?" the man behind the counter asked me.

"Oh, no, *merci beaucoup,*" I replied quickly.

Sophie looked appalled. "Nonsense, *mon amie*, you must try on that sapphire ring. Your father said he would buy you anything you wanted for your thirteenth birthday." Sophie caught my eye and I stifled another giggle.

The man behind the counter suddenly seemed more

interested in helping us. He pulled out an enormous sapphire ring and slipped it on my left ring finger.

I let out a gasp but covered it up with a cough when Sophie poked me in the side. The ring was outrageous … a huge sparkling blue stone. I'd never worn anything so expensive in my entire life.

"Ah! Look at the time." Sophie pointed to a clock on the wall. "We must be going. Thank you so much for your help, *monsieur*," she said, holding out her wrist so he could unclasp the bracelet. I took off the ring and put it back in the box.

"We will have to think about it and come back another day," Sophie told the man, smiling and waving as she hurried out the door.

"*Merci*," I said to the man, who looked quite annoyed, and followed Sophie.

We hurried around the corner before collapsing into a fit of giggles.

"Sophie, I can't believe you … have you done that before?" I asked. I was impressed with her boldness and felt that I must learn to be a little more bold. After all, world travelers can't be shy.

"A few times," she admitted. "But it was the most fun with you here. *Viens*, Charlotte. It really is time to go."

All day long it had rained steadily, and the gutters were filled with water rushing toward the Seine. I looked back a few times, unable to shake the creepy feeling that we were being followed. Sometimes I saw nothing; other

❖

times I could have sworn I caught a glimpse of a brown raincoat. On such a rainy day, there were many men walking around in brown raincoats. *Maybe it wasn't the same man you saw before*, I told myself. *Perhaps I am just being paranoid.*

There were lights on in the houseboat when we returned to the docks, but the curtains were shut, so we couldn't see in. We picked up my pictures at the photo lab and headed back to Sophie's apartment. We were soaked to the bone and exhausted from our long, unsuccessful day of Orangina-hunting.

Even though the day had been fun, I couldn't shake the sinking feeling I had in my stomach. What if it rained like this tomorrow? And on Friday? I might never find Orangina! I had come so far. I couldn't bear the thought of never seeing my orange friend again.

XI

La Découverte

THE DISCOVERY

BY THE TIME WE GOT HOME, both Sophie and I were chilled. I looked like a major fashion disaster—my hair was stringy, my pants were baggy, and my nose was running. Sophie, on the other hand, looked like a chic ad for a raincoat. How did she manage this?

When Madame Morel saw us, she rushed us into the bedroom to change our clothes. After dinner, Sophie settled in to do some homework and I opened up the pictures we'd picked up at the photo lab. They were a little dark, but I could still make out most of them, except the last picture, which didn't turn out too well. It was the darkest of the group—with a blurry band across the middle. There was an artistic quality about it that reminded me of some of the paintings at the Picasso museum. It was so interesting that I decided to save the strange photo to show Isabel when I got home. She would definitely appreciate my accidental artwork.

"It was the sketch of a woman, beautifully depicted in bright shapes and colors."   ~ pg. 136

Now that we were back at Sophie's, I was anxious to email the BSG. I was sure that they would love to hear all about the wonderful museums, our adventure at the jewelry store, and my missing bag. But as soon as I started writing, I felt guilty that I had been enjoying Paris too much. Suddenly, it dawned on me that my stay in Paris was more than half over and there was still no sign of Orangina. This wasn't really a vacation. It was supposed to be a quest, and even though I was having fun I felt like I wasn't working hard enough. What if I never even got a glimpse of Orangina? I was about to ask Sophie again if she was sure she really saw Orangina, but I saw her head bent over her homework.

Everyone complained about the homework at Abigail Adams Junior High, but going to school in Paris was much worse—in France, kids had almost twice the amount of homework. I tried to be quiet while Sophie worked, since I knew how much she had to do. I wrote in my journal for a while and then looked at the calendar I'd bought for Isabel. I couldn't wait to tell her everything I'd learned about Picasso at the museum that day.

That reminded me ... for the first time since I left Boston, I got out the coloring book Isabel had given me. As I opened it, I noticed there was a loose picture inserted in the middle of the pages. Encased in a stiff, old mat, it looked out of place amidst the other shiny photos in the book. *How odd! Where did this come from*? I wondered why I'd never noticed it before.

The picture looked so familiar to me. I examined it more carefully. It was a sketch of a woman, beautifully depicted with bright shapes and colors. Had I seen it at the Picasso museum that day? I really wanted to interrupt Sophie to ask her, but her head was bent over her notebook and she was scribbling away. I looked through Isabel's Picasso calendar again to see if I could find it, but it wasn't there.

My curiosity eventually got the better of me, and I tapped Sophie on the shoulder and showed her the picture. "Sophie, do you remember this picture from the museum?" I handed her the sketch.

She took the picture and studied it. "*Non*, I don't think I've seen this before. Where did you get it?"

"It was stuck inside the Picasso coloring book that Isabel gave me before I left … you know, the one I was telling you about? It must be a little freebie or giveaway or something."

Sophie laughed. "*C'est quoi* 'freebie'? That is a very funny word."

"Just like it sounds," I replied. "Something that costs nothing, something you get for free. A *freebie*," I pronounced, trying to imagine I was hearing the word for the first time. I guess it did sound kind of funny.

"Hmm." Sophie turned her attention back to the picture. "*C'est bizarre*, odd … this paper looks so old and faded, Charlotte. It doesn't look new."

"It's strange," I agreed. "Maybe they were trying to make it look authentic. It looks familiar, though. It's almost as if I've seen this same picture somewhere before.

You're sure you don't remember it?"

Sophie shook her head.

"I'll email Isabel … maybe she'll know more about it."

I signed on and wrote a quick email while Sophie continued her homework.

```
To: Isabel
From: Charlotte
Subject: Picasso Picture

Isabel,
I found a Picasso picture stuck inside
the coloring book you gave me.
Is it a special giveaway or something?
Do all the coloring books have them?
Just asking because this one is familiar
and I can't figure out why. It also
looks old ...
like they were trying to make it look
authentic.
I love the coloring book ... thanx again!
can't wait to tell u all about the
Picasso Museum.
it was really cool!

XOXO
Charlotte
```

It had been so wet in Paris that I wondered what the weather was like back in Boston. I went to *The Boston Globe* website to check, and as I glanced at the homepage, again the word "Picasso" caught my eye.

I clicked on the link to the article and a picture of the missing sketch popped onto the screen. Although I loved to write, sometimes I thought about becoming a detective when I grew up. Being a detective meant paying close attention to all the details and putting the pieces of the puzzle together ... I'm good at that kind of thing. Maybe Katani could even design an investigator outfit for me— complete with a trench coat. For now, I just had to wonder ... how would real detectives ever crack "The Case of the Stolen Picasso Sketch"?

I scanned the article to see if there were any new developments and then looked more carefully at the image of the stolen sketch. A sketch of a lovely woman.

I looked down at the picture in my hand.

I looked back at the picture on the screen.

I looked back and forth, back and forth between the picture in my hand and the picture on the screen.

They were EXACTLY the same.

I gasped and my hands began to tremble. Could it be that I was holding an original Picasso drawing that could be worth millions of dollars? And, if so, how did it get here? It all seemed too weird to be true. But then again ... what if it were?

XII

C'est Vrai?

IS IT TRUE?

SOPHIE AND I STUDIED *The Boston Globe* story that I'd printed out.

"Let's review the facts," I said, getting into my investigative reporter state of mind. As a feature writer for *The Sentinel*, I was used to gathering information and making sense of it all so I could write my articles. "Number one: The sketch was stolen on Friday night. Number two: Isabel bought the coloring book Saturday morning—the morning AFTER the sketch was stolen. Perhaps it was in the coloring book when Isabel bought it."

Sophie picked up the sketch and stared at it. "A thief put a valuable Picasso sketch in a coloring book? *Je ne comprends pas …*"

"I don't understand either. Maybe someone else was supposed to buy it—a 'fence'—you know, someone who deals stolen goods." I'd read enough detective books to know the lingo. "Or maybe the thief was being followed and he needed to hide it quickly, and the book was the easiest place to stash it."

"Charlotte—*quelle imagination*! We do not know if this is a real Picasso—if it is the one in the newspaper article. You are probably right, *mon amie*. It is a free picture—how did you say—a costie?" Sophie asked.

"A freebie. But this all seems too crazy to be just a coincidence. Like you said, it looks old. Besides … it says right here in the article that it was a 'previously unknown, un-catalogued sketch.' How could a copy have been made? This *has* to be the original," I reasoned.

"Oh, Charlotte. *Ce n'est pas vrai*—it can't be true. I truly do not think a thief would put something so valuable in a coloring book," Sophie declared. "It's after school now back home, *n'est-ce pas*? Why don't you check your email? I'm sure Isabel will tell you it was a *freebie*." Sophie emphasized the new English word I taught her.

I logged on to my email account and my heart thumped rapidly as I clicked on a reply from Isabel.

```
To: Charlotte
From: Isabel
Subject: re: Picasso Picture


Charlotte—
i'm embarrassed to tell you this!
but i bought the same Picasso coloring
book for myself when i bought yours
```

(I couldn't resist!).

i checked it.

not sure what u mean about a freebie

... there isn't anything in it at all.

hope that helps!!!!!!!!!!!!

XOXO,

Isabel

P.S. Did you find your cat yet?

I gulped. Not only had I not found my cat, but I apparently had a real live Picasso drawing in my hands. The email clinched it. Sophie read over my shoulder, and her silence told me she too was finally convinced that something very strange was going on.

I cleared my throat and tried to remain calm. "OK. So most likely, the sketch wasn't in the coloring book when Isabel bought it. The question is how did it get there?"

"Where have you taken the book since you got it?" Sophie asked.

"It was on my lap on the plane. Besides that, it was in my messenger bag until I took it out and left it in your room on Monday. Right before the bag was stolen."

"Did you ask anyone to carry your bag for you while you were traveling?"

"No. Of course not."

"Think, Charlotte ... it would have taken only a moment to slip the picture in the book."

"Well, I definitely carried it onto the plane myself. But Mr. Peckham—"

Sophie's eyes widened. "*Oui*! And what about this man, this Mr. Peckham?"

"He helped me put it in the overhead bin. He's the sweetest old man though, like a grandfather. He's a friend of Madame Giroux's. She goes out to dinner at his pub all the time. Mr. Peckham's just a normal, regular guy. There's no way he could be an art thief."

"Did he tell you why he was in Boston?"

"He said he was on vacation … on holidays."

"I see," Sophie said, and then paused for a moment to think. "But didn't Mr. Peckham say he once met Picasso?"

"Yes."

"Wasn't he the one who said he saw Picasso sketching in a pub?"

"Yes …"

"Hmmm. Let me see the sketch again." Sophie carefully slid the thin piece of paper from the protection of the mat and examined it.

"Charlotte! Look at this!"

I looked over her shoulder, and there, right on the back of the sketch, was a bar bill from the Churchill Pub.

For the next hour, Sophie and I argued about Harold G. Peckham, Esquire.

"You must tell someone! Don't you see? He's a thief! A scoundrel!" Sophie insisted.

I didn't know what to think. Maybe Sophie was right.

Mr. Peckham had to be involved with this mess, even if he wasn't the thief. It was too much of a coincidence. He was in Boston when the sketch was stolen. He told me about watching Pablo Picasso sketch at the Churchill Pub, so I know he was familiar with this picture—a "previously unknown" work of art that almost no one else knew about. He had put my coloring book back in my messenger bag at the end of our flight. There would have been enough time for him to quickly slip the sketch into the book. But I couldn't get over the fact that he seemed so nice, so sweet and genuine. Why would he do such a thing? And, if he was the crook, why did he tell me all about his connection to Picasso? Surely if he were an accomplished thief he wouldn't want to leave a trail. It just didn't add up.

"There is something missing here," I said.

"Yes. The missing sketch! You must go *à la gendarmerie*— to the police!"

"The police? No! What if they think I did it?"

Sophie shook her head. "Not if you explain the whole story. Oh, Charlotte! It's your only choice. You can't take it back to Boston."

"I know. I don't want to keep it any longer than I have to. What if someone steals my bag again?"

"Your bag! That explains it! Mr. Peckham! *He* stole your bag." Sophie was convinced.

"What? No way! He wouldn't do that to me. And he doesn't know where you live, anyway … the person who stole my bag must have been following us around these past few days."

"And what makes you think Mr. Peckham wasn't the man following us around? Didn't you say that the suspicious man at Berthillon looked like Mr. Peckham? Charlotte, you are too soft-hearted. You *must* turn him in!" Sophie insisted.

"He must have thought the coloring book with the sketch in it was still in the bag," I said softly. "But it wasn't … it was in your room the whole time. He brought the bag back with everything in it, though. He didn't take a cent. Does that sound like a thief to you?" I asked.

Neither Sophie nor I could answer that question. It was all so confusing, and it was really late and we were getting tired. We decided to wait until morning to decide what to do. Sophie fell asleep right away. I, on the other hand, was wide awake. I stared out the window at the full moon. My heart was racing. What was going on? All I'd wanted to do was come to Paris, find Orangina, and visit with Sophie, and now I was embroiled in an international art theft. This was too much! What was I going to do?

I took out my flashlight and compared *The Boston Globe* article to some of my journal entries. The real owner of the sketch, Mr. Doyle, was originally from Staithes, England. Mr. Peckham had said he was from England—I looked back in my journal—Staithes. Mr. Peckham was from Staithes, too. He said that Staithes was a very small town. The two men must have known each other.

I thought about Mr. Peckham and how kind he had

been to me. I thought of his thick white hair and his neatly trimmed mustache. Something pinged inside of me. I knew all of the evidence added up to Mr. Peckham being the thief, but I wasn't yet willing to believe that he was a criminal. But I knew one thing: there was a mystery to be solved.

Charlotte's Journal

I have a real Picasso sketch—a famous work of art—lying right next to me in Sophie's room at this moment. I'm sure of it. I think it's been with me during this whole trip, and I didn't even know it. It's kind of funny, actually. We've spent the past few days searching everywhere for Orangina, and then out of the blue we found something HUGE that everyone else in the world is looking for. What if I hadn't opened up the Picasso coloring book until I got back to Boston? What if I had been searched at the airport and they found the sketch and thought that I STOLE it? I could only imagine calling my dad from prison to tell him I was involved in an international scandal. So much for being careful and "staying out of trouble." The BSG would have to visit me behind bars. And what about Marty ... do they let dogs make jail visits?

The biggest question of all ... why did Mr. Peckham get involved in this? I just can't believe that he's a bad person. I know Sophie thinks it's silly that I won't immediately turn him in to the police. But first I need to get to the bottom of this. I want to know the truth ... whatever that is.

~ XIII ~

Perdu et Trouvé

LOST AND FOUND

THE NEXT MORNING, I filled Sophie in on the connection between the owner of the sketch—Mr. Doyle—and Mr. Peckham. "But I still don't believe he's a cold-hearted criminal," I told her.

"What does it matter?" Sophie asked. "A thief is a thief is a thief." Sophie was a no nonsense girl—just like Katani. They would probably be high-fiving each other right now.

At least we agreed on one thing: We needed to return the painting before anything happened to it. I didn't want to risk losing it—or more importantly, be accused of stealing it myself! We were both afraid that the police might keep us captive all day long asking questions, so we decided it would be best to take the sketch directly to the Picasso Museum. After all, they were the experts—they would definitely know what to do.

We packed up and rushed through the narrow, historic streets of the Marias until we were standing in front of the

Picasso Museum. I stamped my foot in frustration—it was closed. I looked nervously around, hoping no one had followed us. We waited outside for what seemed like forever. When the doors finally opened at 9 a.m. Sophie and I rushed to the information desk, where I asked to speak to the director. The woman behind the counter asked what it was regarding and Sophie replied authoritatively, "It's a matter of extreme urgency, *Madame*."

The woman's raised eyebrow and icy glare told us she didn't believe a word we were saying. Nonetheless, she ushered us into the director's office a few minutes later.

"*Excusez moi*, I won't take up much of your time," I told the director, a man in a gray suit with a long, thin face, as my palms sweated and my heart thumped. I took the coloring book out of my messenger bag. "You know the missing Picasso sketch that was taken from Boston earlier in the week?" I purposely didn't say the word "stolen."

"*Oui*, I have read the reports. *C'est une tragédie*! Such a tragedy in the art world."

"I believe that this might be the sketch," I said, gingerly placing the sketch on the desk in front of the director. "I found it in a Picasso coloring book my friend bought for me on Saturday in Boston, the day after the robbery. I wanted to make sure it was returned to the rightful owner."

The museum director picked up the sketch and looked at it intently for a few seconds before hitting the buzzer on the desk.

"Yes?" answered a voice from another room.

✤

"Ask DuBon to come here immediately," the director said. Then, he looked up at me suspiciously. "Tell me where you found this again?"

Remembering how confident Sophie had been in the jewelry store, I gathered up all my courage and repeated in a very strong voice what I had just told him. Maybe too strong, as he raised his eyebrows at me when I spoke. "It was in a coloring book my friend bought for me at a store in Boston. The store is only a few miles from where the Picasso sketch was taken," I added.

Sophie nudged me with her elbow and I pushed her arm away. I knew what she was getting at. I made it seem like the sketch had been in the coloring book all along. I just couldn't bring myself to get poor Mr. Peckham into trouble. After all, I wasn't *positive* he was the one who stole the sketch. And the important thing was that the sketch was being returned to its rightful owner. I crossed my fingers and hoped that I wouldn't get in trouble either. By the look on the director's face, I wasn't sure that I would be so lucky.

Another very serious-looking man entered the room. The two museum experts examined the sketch carefully and whispered to each other.

I nervously stood up to leave. "I just wanted to make sure it was safely returned—if it is the real missing sketch."

The director assured me he would take care of it and asked me to leave my name, U.S. address, and French address. Sophie wrote everything down in French for me.

The day suddenly seemed so much brighter when we

walked outside.

I took a deep breath, feeling as if a huge weight had been lifted. Still, I didn't feel like it was over. There were too many unanswered questions.

"Charlotte, you made it sound like the sketch was in the coloring book BEFORE you flew to Paris. Why did you do that?" Sophie asked.

I didn't answer, but Sophie could read my face.

"Why are you protecting that man anyway?"

I shrugged. The truth was I didn't know why. I just felt that *if* Mr. Peckham did take the sketch ... it was for reasons other people might not understand.

"Charlotte! I'm *très serieuse*. Why are you protecting him?" a clearly exasperated Sophie asked again.

"I'm not sure ..." I told her honestly. Maeve always said I was a softie. Was I too much of a softie? Was I protecting a dangerous criminal? "The important thing is that the sketch will be returned to its rightful owner."

I thought Sophie might be angry with me, but she just shrugged her shoulders and let the whole thing drop. That was why we were friends. Even if we didn't always agree, we somehow understood each other.

"Maybe you're right, Charlotte. Now what?" she asked. I had forgotten how practical Sophie could be. It was a very reassuring quality in a friend.

"Let's forget about criminals. Time's running out. We have only two days left to find Orangina. Let's go!"

~ XIV ~

~ XIV ~

Pas Une Minute à Perdre

THE CLOCK IS TICKING

WE WALKED QUICKLY back to the river. The day was gray, but not wet. I was grateful it wasn't raining. As we strolled slowly along the quay, the traffic on nearby streets increased. Today there were cats everywhere we looked—black cats, white cats, cats with long bushy tails, cats with short stubby tails. One or two fat cats and lots of skinny, hungry-looking cats.

St-Germain was covered with plaques honoring all the Americans who had been there before us: John Paul Jones, Benjamin Franklin, John Jay, and John Adams from the Colonial days. There were also the writers, like Gertrude Stein and James Baldwin. I loved Gertrude Stein's famous quote, *"Rose is a rose is a rose is a rose."*

"Charlotte, maybe someday there will be a plaque down by the quay that says, 'Pulitzer Prize-winning author Charlotte Ramsey once lived on a houseboat on the River Seine,'" mused Sophie as she grabbed my arm.

There are hundreds of narrow, winding streets throughout Paris. I've always loved the blue-and-white street signs and the colorful names, too—rue des Mauvais-Garçons (Bad Boys' Street), rue du Chat-Qui Pêche (Fishing Cat Street), rue des Quatre Vents (Street of the Four Winds), and so on.

"Wouldn't it be great if we found Orangina on Fishing Cat Street?" I asked Sophie.

"Yes ... we'd have to get our picture taken with Orangina in front of the street sign."

I began laughing and then stopped and frowned. The search was getting desperate. I had gone from thinking about "when" we would find Orangina to "if" we would ever find him.

It was noon by the time we worked our way back to the houseboat. I felt as hungry as one of those skinny cats we'd seen wandering around. We had lunch at a small café and then headed upriver for a change of scenery. Le Quai Malaquais was full of people heading to and from class at the beautiful École des Beaux-Arts, the most well-renowned school of fine arts in France. We wandered about the sculpture garden next to the art school, hoping we might spot Orangina prowling around a statue there.

Even though the day was gray, the sidewalk that curved through the sculpture garden was full of activity. Some people walked, while others skated by on rollerblades. Students had decorated some of the sculptures with pieces of clothing or draped them in exotic fabrics. One statue even had on sunglasses. It was good to see that people could have a sense of humor about art.

On our way back toward the houseboat that evening, we stopped at Square du Vert-Galant. This small square—it's a triangle, really—was tucked beneath le Pont-Neuf. It was hidden from the view of the traffic above. Benches lined the grass, and there were great views of l'Ile de la Cité and l'Ile St-Louis. After another long, disappointing search, Sophie and I sat silently soaking in the final light of the day.

And then I had to ask … "Sophie … are you sure that you saw Orangina? Do you think maybe it was a look-alike?" I asked gingerly, glancing over at my friend.

"I *know* it was him, Charlotte. I know it! I would never have said something to you if I was not sure. He was still wearing that collar we bought for him at the pet store."

"I'm so sorry." I looked down and shook my head. "I didn't mean to doubt you, it's just that I'm losing hope."

"*Je sais*, I know. And you weren't doubting me, just … checking." Sophie smiled.

The clouds opened up and the sun peeked through. It had been a long, exhausting day of walking, but somehow seeing the sun shining made up for it. That was the thing about Paris—the beauty of the city always snuck up to surprise you.

~ XV ~

Une Dernière Chance

ONE LAST CHANCE

IT WAS FRIDAY, my last full day in Paris. My last chance to find Orangina and bring him home. My last day with Sophie. I could tell by her eyes that she was sad that I was leaving. It was like we had been sisters for the week—living in the same bedroom, sharing parents, eating together, hunting for Orangina. The two of us were quiet as we walked down to the dock and stood once again in front of the houseboat.

"What if we don't find him?" I asked softly.

"We will look hard today," Sophie assured me. "Do not give up yet, Charlotte."

"You don't think something happened to him?"

"No. Of course not!" Sophie said. "Orangina is a smart cat … wise. He knows the streets. You can see it in his eyes. He found you, didn't he? He knows how to take care of himself." I gratefully squeezed Sophie's hand.

I was on edge that morning. I hadn't slept much and

was nervous about finding Orangina, but there was something else too. Something that I couldn't quite put my finger on.

It was raining again for our final search. I made a mental note to make my next trip to Paris in the springtime! Sophie and I decided not to venture too far from the houseboat this time. The two of us split up, each walking a half hour in the opposite direction and back again. That way we could cover more area in a shorter amount of time. I stopped at every alleyway and called out to Orangina. At one stop, a little gray cat came bounding out from behind a can. I bent over and offered it a few of the nibbles I had stashed in my pocket. As I wandered on I could feel my frustration building. At one point I yelled at the top of my lungs, "Orangina, you naughty cat, come out, come out wherever you are!" No response except for an ornery old woman who yelled out of her window for me to be quiet.

"*Pardonez moi!*" I called quickly and scurried on. My father's voice rang in my ears that no one should be rude, especially in a foreign country where you were a guest. I walked on past a shop with the most delicious looking pastries, but I wasn't even tempted. The realization that I might never see Orangina again had completely ruined my appetite.

Sophie and I met back at the houseboat just before noon.

She insisted that we grab a quick lunch of tuna sandwiches. "*Tu dois manger.* You must eat, Charlotte. You need to keep your energy going for our final push." I laughed and gave her a salute. Sophie had sounded like a French general marshalling her troops.

After lunch, we wandered aimlessly down le Boulevard St-Germain and turned on la rue de Buci to where it intersected with la rue de Seine. We stumbled across le Marché Buci, an open-air food market. Crowded into a small area were hundreds of food stalls full of the best fruits, vegetables, breads, meats, fish, and cheeses in Paris. The smell was overpowering. For a chef, going to that market would be like landing in heaven.

We carefully threaded our way through the crowd. The voices of the merchants followed us everywhere. *"Regardez mesdames, mademoiselles, messieurs!"* one woman chanted. Another woman across the way sang out, *"Deux euros pour trois, deux euros pour trois."*

The dairy stands were piled high with huge wheels of cheese, baskets of eggs, and giant crocks of creamy butter. The women that worked in the cheese booths wore white smocks and tied their hair back with white kerchiefs.

At a vegetable stand across from the largest cheese stall, a scraggly looking farmer in a red sweater caught my eye. He wore a green apron and a cap pulled low on his brow. He scowled at a man who disturbed his tomato display. As soon as the offending man left, the farmer rushed to rearrange his tomatoes. Then he grabbed a broom and swept the floor with intense, angry jabs, almost bumping into a woman looking at cucumbers. I thought for a moment he was trying to sweep her away from his vegetable stall.

"We call him *mauvais Caractère*—Sourpuss," Sophie whispered in my ear. "He never has a kind word for anyone. He is successful only because his vegetables are the best in the market."

I smiled and thought of Yuri, who ran the fruit stand in my neighborhood at home … how underneath his gruff exterior, he had a heart of gold. Maybe it was the same with *mauvais Caractère*, the Sourpuss.

We continued on through le Marché Buci past stands of fresh fish, stalls stacked with dry goods, blooming flower stalls, and colorful fruit stands. Instead of looking at the wares the vendors were selling, I kept my eyes low, watching for the tip of a stiff, proud tail.

"I don't know where else to look," I said helplessly to Sophie as we left le Marché Buci.

"Come," she said. "Let's take a break and do some shopping of our own. You still have one gift left to buy, no? For *la petite* Avery?"

"But Sophie," I protested. "Time is running out."

"Charlotte," she answered firmly. "We are doing our very best. Paris is a huge city. *Une très grande ville*! Orangina could be anywhere."

I nodded sadly. I knew she was right. Orangina was probably lost forever to me. I brushed a tear from my eye and followed Sophie down into the *métro*.

We traveled four stops, and when we came up there were people everywhere. Groups of women chattered as they shopped. Grandmothers pushed strollers. Mothers held onto toddlers' hands. Dogs big and small tugged on their leashes ... I'd forgotten how Parisians adore their dogs. Marty would love walking around the streets of Paris, stopping to sniff at all the pastry crumbs and running around and around in the grassy park by the Eiffel Tower.

"Welcome to the 'Attic of Paris,'" Sophie said, gesturing around her. "They have everything you could ever imagine—paintings, antique furniture, mirrors, silk fabrics, crystal vases, porcelain figurines, costume jewelry, toys, recycled clothes, handbags, luggage. There has to be something here for Avery."

As we pushed our way through this market, I kept my eyes open for two things—a gift for Avery and any stray cats wandering around. I couldn't help myself. I didn't want to give up on Orangina. It's hard to give up on something that you want with all of your heart. Perhaps, if I crossed my fingers and wished with all my might. ... Suddenly, I caught a glimpse of a man in a yellow raincoat and hat. I took a few steps closer to get a better look, but he disappeared behind a noisy group of people.

Now that was interesting, I realized. I hadn't seen a suspicious man in a raincoat and hat since my messenger bag was stolen. Was the man in the raincoat really Harold G. Peckham, Esquire? Was he *still* following me through the streets of Paris? If so, why?

I didn't say anything about it to Sophie. I knew she would immediately call Mr. Peckham a thief again and then insist we should alert the police. I wasn't sure that it was him anyway. After all, I reasoned, it was raining and there must be a zillion French men in raincoats. Besides, I still wasn't ready to turn in Mr. Peckham. My instincts told me that there was more to this story. And I just had to find out what it was.

But first, I needed to find a gift for Avery. As usual, Sophie came to the rescue and spied a French World Cup Soccer T-shirt. It was perfect. I was sure Avery would love it! When I found out it only cost five euros I was ecstatic. There was nothing like a bargain. Now all the Beacon Street Girls would have mementos from the trip. I only wished that I could have my *souvenir*—a fuzzy, orange *souvenir* to be exact. I sighed. Hope dies hard.

We started walking back to the docks in silence. The light was fading on my last full day in Paris. I knew in my heart that I would have to return home without Orangina.

Sophie could sense what I was thinking. "Don't worry, Charlotte. I will keep looking," she said softly.

I swallowed and nodded. For a moment I thought I might cry. I'd been hoping with all my might to find my precious Orangina. And in whatever spare moments I wasn't thinking about my poor cat, I couldn't help but wonder about poor Mr. Peckham, who might end up in jail. Suddenly, I knew what I had to do. I had to find him. If I couldn't find Orangina, I could at least solve the mystery of Mr. Peckham. I needed to understand why he did what he did. That way, I could finally put together the missing pieces of the puzzle. I explained this to Sophie as we slowly, solemnly walked back to my old houseboat one last time.

"Well, *mon amie*, as much as I think you should not have sympathy for that man … I will support you. And, of course, you will not go alone to find him. I'll be with you the whole time … just in case."

"Thanks, Soph. I knew I could count on you. Besides, I don't think anything will happen to us. We will figure out how to talk to him in a safe place. Don't worry, OK?"

Sophie nodded but she gave me a funny look. I don't think Sophie enjoyed detective work like I did, but she was trying her best to be a good sport. That was a nice quality to have in a friend.

As I stood in front of the houseboat, I could hear the traffic sounds drifting over from distant streets and the constant creaking of the ropes as boats bobbed in the water.

"I can't believe my week in Paris is over. It went by in an instant."

"I wish you could stay longer …"

"Me too. It's been so much fun! I just wish I had seen Orangina. I didn't even get a glimpse of him."

Sophie grabbed my hand and squeezed it. "I promise you I will keep looking for him," she reassured me. "I will walk along the Seine and call for him, 'Orangina, you naughty thing, come out wherever you are!'"

I had to laugh, and I was surprised that Sophie was a combination of Katani and Maeve. Orderly and organized and dramatic all at the same time.

✤

I looked out onto the steel gray waters of the Seine and took a deep breath. The light was fading fast, and a low, misty, swirling fog was forming over the surface of the river. I heard the *putt-putt* of a motor and looked up as a barge appeared under the bridge. "Oh my goodness!" I gasped and squeezed Sophie's hand as hard as I could. I couldn't believe it. For there, on the front of the last barge of the day — the barge filled with vegetables, was a spot of orange fur glowing through the fog. I was so stunned, all I could manage to do was continue to squeeze Sophie's hand and point.

"Orangina!" Sophie cried.

That wily cat was sitting proudly at the front of the barge, as if he was the captain of a great ship, steering it wherever he wanted to go.

"It is him! It is truly him!" Sophie exclaimed, pointing toward the barge.

"ORANGINA!" I yelled out.

Orangina meowed loudly at the sound of his name. He looked at me for a moment, blinked, and I swear, that crazy cat smiled. Then he turned his face back to the wind as the barge slid under a low bridge and continued its way up river.

"*Regarde! Regarde!* Charlotte! See who is at the motor? It is him. It is *mauvais Caractère*, the Sourpuss!"

Sure enough, there, operating the motor, was the same grouchy farmer from le Marché Buci. He'd taken off his green apron, but he had on the same red sweater and cap pulled low over his eyes. I squinted to get a better look at his face. Was it just my imagination, or had a slight grin replaced his signature scowl?

"Come on!" I yelled. "Let's go!"

I ran by the river trying to follow the barge. I had come this far, I was not about to give up yet. Breathing hard, I watched as Orangina made his way along the edge of Sourpuss's barge. He was calling out to me. My heart leapt at the sound of his distinctive howl. But just then the barge made its way under another bridge and I ran into a gate that would not open. I jiggled frantically at the latch, but it was stuck. I stamped my foot in frustration as I witnessed Orangina promenade down next to the farmer, who tossed him a scrap of something to eat. After one last howl, Orangina and the barge passed around a bend in the river. In an instant, Orangina was gone.

Sophie and I stood in silence, panting as the wake of the barge sloshed against the dock. I didn't know what to think. Orangina was alive. Alive and healthy. I hated to admit it, but he really looked happy with the Sourpuss. And the Sourpuss looked happy with him. I smiled. Orangina was obviously a survivor. Who knew where that cat would end up? I had a sudden vision of him traveling all around the world—maybe even to India and China. I had a funny feeling that I would run into Orangina again.

"Now we know where to find him, Charlotte!" an excited Sophie clapped her hands. "The Sourpuss is at le Marché Buci every day. I will go there tomorrow after school. Perhaps I can send Orangina on a plane to you tomorrow. The next plane after you! You could wait for him at the airport."

I looked at Sophie and grabbed her hands. It was at that moment that I knew the truth. "Sophie," I said, "Orangina belongs to the Seine with its barges and fish, just the same way I now belong back in Brookline in the yellow Victorian with my dad and Miss Pierce and Marty."

Sophie stared at me, tears forming in the corner of her eyes. "But Charlotte, you and Orangina are both Parisians … how can you …?" Sophie was struggling for words.

"Sophie, that's the point. Orangina is a Paris cat. I hope you visit him and give him bits of fish for me. But I am an American girl now. I can't bring a Paris cat to live in America. He just wouldn't be happy."

"But …" she protested.

"Don't worry, Sophie," I assured her. "A piece of my heart is in Paris, and I will always come back to visit you and Orangina."

Sophie smiled. That's all she needed to hear—that I would always be her friend, and that I would never forget our wonderful adventures together.

I gave Sophie a huge hug and then looked at my watch. "It's getting late. We have to find Mr. Peckham soon … it's my last chance to get to the bottom of this."

★

Sophie and I headed back to her apartment to come up with a plan. No one else was home when we arrived, but Sophie's parents would be back in another hour or so. That meant we would have to move quickly.

"Where will we find him?" Sophie asked.

"The Churchill Pub," I replied. "It's Friday, late afternoon … he has to be there. Friday nights are really busy for restaurants. Everybody wants to celebrate the end of the week."

"What if he tries to kidnap us?" Sophie asked.

"We won't go anywhere alone with him," I said. "We'll walk into the restaurant, ask to speak with him, and make him talk to us right then and there. In front of everyone. I looked up the address online. It happens to be right next to *la gendarmerie,* so if we feel unsafe, we could go there right away."

Sophie looked a little pale but she nodded in agreement. I was actually excited for our little adventure. I felt like Nancy Drew or Sherlock Holmes.

"Hold on, Sophie. I just need a few minutes to think about what I'm going to say to Mr. Peckham," I explained to Sophie, who already had her coat on.

I plopped down on the floor of Sophie's room with all the evidence spread out around me—the coloring book, my journal, the printed news article, the picture of the sketch from *The Boston Globe* website. I twirled my pen around in my hand and rested my head against Sophie's bed for a few seconds, reliving my conversations with Mr.

Peckham. I opened up to a blank page in my journal and made a list of the facts about the man in question. *He owns the Churchill Pub. He's lived in Paris for years and years. He is not married but he loved a woman named Agnes once.*

I snatched up the news article and scanned it again. The owner of the Picasso sketch, Mr. Doyle, said that Picasso had sketched his wife, who had died earlier in the year. I paged through my journal until I found where I had written it down that Agnes, whose picture Mr. Peckham carried, had died last June.

I shut my eyes and tried to remember the picture in Mr. Peckham's wallet. Agnes had dark hair, a simple, flowing dress, and hypnotic eyes that turned down at the ends, which made her look sad and happy at the same time. I looked at the printout of the stolen Picasso sketch. There was something about the woman's eyes ... they had the same hypnotic quality I remembered from the photo of Agnes.

"Sophie!" I snapped my fingers. "*Allons-y*—let's go!!"

Face à Face

FACE-TO-FACE

TO SAVE TIME, we took a taxi to the Churchill Pub. I didn't breathe a word to Sophie about what I thought I'd just figured out—I wanted to hear the whole truth from Mr. Peckham first.

When we pushed through the door, the first thing I saw was a man with thick, white hair standing behind the bar. Sophie hung behind at the door while I marched up to the bar.

"Excuse me, Mr. Peckham. I was wondering if I could talk to you," I said assertively.

Mr. Peckham turned toward me and jumped when he realized who it was. "Wh-why Charlotte! What a surprise! Whatever are you doing here?"

"I came to talk to you about the sketch."

His eyes widened. "Sketch? Uh … um," he stuttered, obviously flustered. "What sketch?"

"The Picasso. The one you slipped into my coloring

book on the plane."

"I am so sorry. I have absolutely no idea what you're talking about," he said, nervously looking toward the door.

"I know you took the sketch, Mr. Peckham. I already returned it to the museum. It's the sketch you talked about, isn't it? The one you saw Picasso draw right here at the Churchill Pub?"

Mr. Peckham's eyes darted around the pub as if he was expecting the police to jump out and arrest him any second.

"Mr. Peckham," I said. "I haven't told anyone yet that it was you. I let the museum director think it was in the coloring book when my friend bought it."

Mr. Peckham pulled a handkerchief out of his front pocket and mopped his forehead, which was suddenly beaded with sweat.

"Perhaps we should talk over here," he said, pointing toward an empty table.

"My friend Sophie is here too," I told him and pointed to Sophie. "You know, the one I told you about." I motioned for Sophie to sit down with us at the table.

"Would you young ladies like a soft drink? An *Orangina*?" Mr. Peckham asked. He really was a very polite man.

I nodded. Mr. Peckham motioned to a waitress and ordered two *Orangina* sodas for the both of us.

"You say the sketch has been returned?" he asked when the waitress left.

I nodded.

"And there were ... uh ... no questions ... about me?"

I shook my head no.

"I don't know how to thank you. I ... once I took it, I ... well ... ever since, I've been a nervous wreck."

"You were so nice to me on the plane, but still ... you stole something. And you brought me into this mess by hiding the sketch in my coloring book, putting me in potential danger. It wasn't until this afternoon that I put all the pieces together. That sketch ... it's Agnes, isn't it?"

Both Mr. Peckham and Sophie looked at me in complete and total amazement.

"Why ... yes. But Charlotte, my dear ... how ever did you know?"

"Remember, you showed me the picture of Agnes. The newspaper article said that the Picasso sketch was of Mr. Doyle's wife, who died earlier this year. You told me that Agnes died this year. I knew that you and Mr. Doyle were from the same town in England ... Staithes. On the plane you got so angry when you were talking about the man who stole Agnes from you. And there's something about Agnes's eyes ... I noticed how beautiful they were when you showed me her picture. Picasso captured them perfectly in his sketch. Am I right?" I asked him.

"Charlotte, you are quite right ... a most perceptive young lady. A regular sleuth, I'd say. Quite impressive."

"So, you didn't take it for money. You took it because it was a memory of the woman you loved," I concluded.

Mr. Peckham continued in a low tone. "Yes. Doyle was

going to sell the sketch. That picture was her very essence and he was going to sell it. He never knew a good thing when he had it. Agnes and I were friends for many years, but I could never summon the courage to tell her I loved her. Then it was too late—she married that despicable Doyle character.

"When I read in the news that a rare Picasso sketch was going on the auction block, well, I couldn't think clearly after that. Before I knew it, I was on a plane to Boston. I found Doyle's address in the phone book. It was really quite easy ... I crawled into his home through an open window. It felt so satisfying to take something from him since he had taken Agnes away from me all those years ago. It wasn't until I was on the plane back to Paris that I came to my senses and realized that what I had done was terribly wrong. My emotions had gotten the better of me. Not only was I wrong, but I could get caught and go to jail for the rest of my life. I declare, whatever was I thinking? I've never done anything even remotely like this in all my years, but my love for her got the better of me. Oh, I'm so ashamed of myself!"

I took a sip of my drink as Mr. Peckham pulled himself together. He was clearly completely distraught over what he had done.

"That's why I hid it in your coloring book. It was the only thing I could think to do at the time. I knew the police would never suspect you. I hoped to get it back from you before you discovered it. When I took your bag and didn't find the coloring book inside … I panicked. I've been waiting for the police to come take me away ever since. Imagine prison at my age. I'm afraid it would undo me!"

I glanced over at Sophie, who was sitting there with her mouth pursed. "Are you the man in the different colored raincoats who was following us all over Paris?" she asked.

Mr. Peckham blushed. "I'm afraid so."

"You really shouldn't do things like that. It wasn't very nice." Sophie spoke calmly but seemed a little less confident than usual.

"Really, Mr. Peckham," I added, "it was kind of creepy."

Mr. Peckham looked mortified. "Please accept my deepest apologies, *Mesdemoiselle*s Sophie and Charlotte. I never meant to do anyone any harm. I can only tell you that the death of my beloved Agnes unhinged me."

Sophie shrugged her shoulders. She was French, after all, and understood the ways *du coeur* — of the heart.

"You have done me a great service, my dear, by returning the sketch without implicating me. I will be forever grateful to you. And I am astonished that you unraveled this mystery. You want to be a writer someday, am I correct? Perhaps you are a budding Agatha Christie?" Mr. Peckham suggested.

I smiled. Mysteries would be fun to write.

"I'm really sorry about the sketch," I told him. "I know how much it meant to you."

"I'm sorry, too, Mr. Peckham," Sophie spoke up.

"When Charlotte insisted you were not a criminal, I didn't believe her. But still, it doesn't seem right that you should get away with this."

I stared at Sophie. Maybe she had a future career in criminal justice.

"You are of course right, *Mademoiselle* Sophie. Would it satisfy your sense of justice if I made a substantial contribution to le Musée Picasso—one that would help the museum to buy the sketch?" Mr. Peckham asked.

Sophie was silent for a moment and then answered, "*C'est bien*—that's good."

Mr. Peckham's shoulders relaxed and he continued. "As much as it meant to me, I am better off without the sketch. I would have been looking over my shoulder all my life and living with a guilty conscience. Although it hurts me to know that Agnes won't be with me … I have to come to terms with the fact that the sketch will not bring her back. It is just one way to remember my dear love."

We talked for a while longer about the events of the week. Mr. Peckham was very amused by the story of seeing Orangina on the barge. "By jove!" he said. "That is a good one."

"I have one more question for you, Mr. Peckham. Did you by any chance take a picture with my disposable camera?" I pulled the strange picture out of my bag.

"Oh, dear." Mr. Peckham took the picture from my hand and looked at it carefully. "When I was searching for the sketch in your bag, I accidentally pressed the camera button. I'm afraid my clumsiness got the better of me yet again. I suppose I wouldn't make a very good criminal after all."

I couldn't help but laugh. "It's OK, Mr. Peckham. I think you're better off being the very nice man you are."

When we finished our *Oranginas*, Mr. Peckham walked us to the door.

"I hope someday our paths cross again," he said.

"I do, too," I agreed.

"And if not, I hope to find your books on the bookshelves in a few years. Somehow I think I will. I sense you have a brilliant future ... as a writer ... or a detective."

Mr. Peckham dug into his pocket and pulled out his keys. He unhooked his favorite key chain and held it out to me. "I would like for you to have my mother's four-leaf clover. I hope it brings you luck in love and life. You brought me luck by doing the right thing with the sketch. Now, the luck will be all yours. You are a bright young woman with a great and generous heart. You will go far."

I took the key chain from his outstretched hand. "Thank you, Mr. Peckham. This is the perfect *souvenir* from my trip to Paris. *Au revoir*."

~ XVII ~

La Soirée

THE PARTY

WE TOOK A TAXI back to Sophie's apartment, hoping that Madame Morel wasn't too worried about us.

"Charlotte … I can't believe you figured out about Mr. Peckham and Agnes and the sketch … you are a wonderful detective!" Sophie exclaimed as we rode home.

"When I put all the facts together, it all made sense. I didn't want to say anything until I heard the truth from Mr. Peckham though. I'm glad he's not mad that we returned the sketch to the museum."

"It *was* the right thing to do," Sophie said. "Even Mr. Peckham said that."

The elevator in Sophie's building was on the top floor, so we decided to take the stairs instead of waiting for it. Some of the older apartment buildings in Paris had little buttons called *la minuterie* that switched on a timed light on the landings and in the hallways. They were made of stuff that glowed a greenish-yellow in the dark. When you pushed the button, the light in the hall or stairwell came on for one minute—that was why they were called *la minuterie*. I swear *les minuteries* in the Morels' apartment house were off by about 45 seconds. I used to have the worst time with them when I lived in Paris—every time I pushed one, I would only get halfway up the stairwell before the light would go out and I would have to feel my way along the staircase until I found the next one. Luckily, Sophie had lots of practice. She expertly pressed the buttons and rushed up the stairs to get to the next before the light went off.

Madame Morel opened the door to the apartment before we had the chance. She must have been listening for us.

"Girls! You are back. I was starting to worry that something had happened to you. Did you have any luck with your search?"

Sophie and I exchanged relieved glances. Neither of us knew what Madame Morel would say if she found out what we'd really been doing for the past couple of hours.

"Yes, we saw Orangina!" Sophie recounted the story of Orangina perched on top of the barge.

"*Formidable*! I'm so glad you girls had a successful day. Somehow, I think that Orangina has, how do you say, *nine lives*. What a perfect end to your visit," Madame observed.

I nodded. Madame Morel didn't know how right she was, considering the other significant events of the day.

"We must get ready for your party now, Charlotte. You don't want to keep *Philippe* waiting," Sophie teased.

✤

I decided to wear my chocolate brown corduroy pants and my light blue sweater. Sophie said the blue sweater made my eyes seem turquoise green. The scarf Madame Morel had bought for me was a perfect match.

"Will you help me with the scarf?" I asked Sophie.

"I think you should wear it in your hair," Sophie decided, holding up the scarf against my head.

"My hair?"

"Brush your hair upside down," Sophie said as she handed me the hairbrush.

I hung my head down and brushed my hair until it was smooth and full. Sophie folded the scarf into a thin strip and positioned it headband-style on my head. She tied an expert knot at the nape of my neck and smoothed my hair back in place.

"Oh, Charlotte, it is just the color for you, *n'est-ce pas*? The brown brings out the highlights in your hair and the blue makes your green eyes shine."

"Your mother said the same thing."

"Oh no! Look at the time. We must hurry!"

We didn't wait for the elevator, but stumbled down the dark staircase. Sophie hit each *minuterie* as she passed. We pushed through the front door into the cool evening air. Up the hill we ran, dodging puddles as we climbed, arriving at Pizza Pino only a few minutes later than we planned.

I was surprised to find the pizza place packed with former classmates, including kids I didn't even think knew I existed. I was most surprised to see Céleste and

Chantal—the Whisperers—there. They probably came because they didn't want to be left out, not because they wanted to spend any time with me or wish me *bon voyage*. I noticed how they checked out my outfit. Before we even sat down for pizza, they were whispering to each other. I wondered what would happen if Anna and Joline ever met Céleste and Chantal.

"Come, Charlotte, sit. We are about to order," Philippe said, scooting over in his booth to make room for me.

I froze right in my tracks … Philippe wanted *me* to sit next to *him*?

Thankfully, Sophie gave me little push from behind, or I might have stood there forever.

"We plan on ordering an American special for our table. One cheese and one pepperoni. Is that all right with you?" Philippe asked.

I nodded, looking at all the people around me. It was nice being with practically the whole class, but kind of strange as well. I don't remember hanging out with everyone at once when I actually lived in Paris.

When the pizza came, we all dug in. After eating amazing French food all week, I was surprised at how deliciously refreshing the pizza tasted … almost as good as Village Fare at home. I smiled. It was nice to know for once where home was.

The kids asked more questions about the United States, and then Alain asked me what I missed most about France.

I didn't even have to think about it. "The Seine," I

replied. It sounded silly to miss a river, but it was true. "And of course, my friends." I glanced sideways at Sophie. She smiled back.

As we finished eating, Philippe asked if I would do him a favor and buy him a Yankees baseball cap when I returned to the United States.

"The Yankees?"

"It is America's favorite baseball team, no?"

"No! Absolutely not. I live in Boston. We're Red Sox fans. Buying a Yankees cap would be ... well, betraying my home team!"

Philippe gave me a quizzical look and I knew that I'd never be able to explain the fierce rivalry between the Red Sox and the Yankees to him. A few months ago, I wouldn't have understood it either.

"I'll take a Red Sox cap then." Philippe lifted his arms in surrender.

"You got it," I grinned.

It was getting late and things were winding down. Sophie scooted out of the booth first. "Oh, Charlotte, I almost forgot. *Maman* asked me to pick up something from the drugstore down the street. Could you meet me at the corner in ten minutes?"

Before I had a chance to reply, she was gone.

"I'll walk you to the corner," Philippe offered.

He helped me put on my new purple coat. I said good-bye to the others and thanked them for coming. I promised to keep in touch and invited them all to visit me in Boston.

The night air was cool. Philippe put his arm around me to keep me warm. I blushed, but I had to remember that I was in France, and here people were much more casual about putting their arms around each other. It was an act of friendship. Philippe asked me what kids were like in America. I couldn't help but giggle. Philippe looked quizzically at me. But how could anyone ever describe the Yurtmeister or Billy Trentini or Maeve and her dramatic ways? I told Philippe that he would have to visit someday and find out for himself.

Sophie, of course, wasn't waiting at the corner when we got there.

"I will wait with you until Sophie arrives so you won't be alone," Philippe said.

"*Merci*, Philippe. That'd be nice." I would miss speaking French when I got back to Boston.

He took a piece of paper from his pocket. "This is my address and email. You will write, no? And send me that cap? Also, to help me practice my English." Then he smiled, and I understood that "practicing English" was just his excuse to keep in touch with me.

"Of course," I stammered, taking the paper from his hand. My fingers brushed against his and my breath caught in my throat.

"I won't say *au revoir*, but instead, *à bientôt*—see you soon. I hope I do see you soon."

I opened my mouth, but nothing came out. I couldn't

✤

think of anything to say in French or English. Some things never change!

Thankfully, Sophie came out of the drugstore just in time, and the two of us waved good-bye to Philippe and walked down the hill toward the apartment together.

Dans Tes Rêves

IN YOUR DREAMS

I WAS EXHAUSTED by the time we arrived back at the Morels' apartment. Sophie had to go to school in the morning after she and her dad dropped me off at the airport, and I had a long trip home, so we turned the lights out and tried to keep our voices low.

We talked about Philippe and Alain and Céleste and Chantal, the *Chuchoteurs*. I told her about the piece of paper Philippe handed me right before she joined us on the corner.

"I know you made up the whole story about getting something for your mother at the drugstore, Sophie. Don't try to deny it. You left us alone together on purpose," I accused her.

"Of course I did, Charlotte. Aren't you glad?" Sophie asked, her eyes twinkling.

"I ... I don't know. You know me ... I couldn't think of anything to say!" I admitted. "Oh wait, I think I promised to give him English lessons ..."

Sophie laughed. "Oh, Charlotte, you are so funny! Promise that you'll keep writing to me all the time. And you must come back to visit Paris soon—I will miss you so much."

"What if you came to Boston sometime?" I asked.

"Actually, that is not such a crazy idea. My father has been dealing with a man named the Cheese Man ... you have heard of him?"

"There's a children's book called *The Stinky Cheeseman*. Is that what you mean?"

Sophie laughed. "No, I am sure not! This man lives in New York and writes a magazine column called 'How Cheese Can Improve Your Life.' Interesting title, no? He is working on a book. My father is helping him with inside information on rare French cheeses."

"So you might come to New York? Boston is so close. You would have to come for a week or more!"

"I would love to meet your friends ... the Beacon Street Girls."

"They'd love to meet you too. I've told them so much about you!"

Just then there was a soft knock at Sophie's bedroom door. "*Bonne nuit* girls," was all Madame Morel said, but the hint was obvious.

Sophie and I were instantly silent. We listened for Madame's footsteps. When we heard her bedroom door open and close, we started talking again, but more quietly this time.

"Tomorrow after school I will go to the Marché Buci and approach the Sourpuss. I will tell him that Orangina belongs to you, and that he better treat him right. I will bring some little fish heads for him. You are right, Charlotte. I think Orangina belongs to the Seine. He looked so happy today … so much at home. And the most important thing is that he is healthy and cared for. Even though the farmer is a Sourpuss, he seems to be taking care of Orangina just fine."

"And who knows?" I told her. "Orangina might not stay with Mr. Sourpuss either. Perhaps he'll get bored and find another home."

"Oh, are you sure? You have come so far to get Orangina back!"

"Orangina wasn't the only reason I came to Paris. He's not the only one it's hard for me to be without. You are such a wonderful friend—almost a sister, really. But like Orangina … you belong in Paris. At least I always know where to find *you*," I confessed with a smile.

"I will miss you very much. You are my best friend," Sophie whispered. "Good night, Charlotte."

As I laid there in the dark with the full moon shining through the window, I thought about everything that had happened that day—seeing Orangina, figuring out why Mr. Peckham stole the sketch, going to the Churchill Pub, Philippe handing me his email address, finding out that Sophie might visit the United States in the near future,

✤

even recognizing that as much as I loved Orangina, the right place for him was just where he was—near the Seine.

I shut my eyes and imagined Sophie climbing the ladder to the Tower. I would show her all my favorite places in my hometown—Montoya's Bakery, Irving's Toy and Card Shop, The Book Nook, and Fenway Park. We would take Marty for a long walk with all of the Beacon Street Girls. With these happy images flickering in my head, I fell fast asleep.

~ XIX ~

A la Prochaine Fois

UNTIL NEXT TIME

NO MATTER WHERE I'VE LIVED, I've always hated to get up early in the morning. And this morning, my last morning in Paris, we had to get up before dawn so that I could make my flight back to Boston. Even so, there was no mad dash. Breakfast seemed soothing, leisurely, as if I had all the time in the world. I knew that I would miss that feeling in America, where everyone always seemed to be in a hurry.

Monsieur Morel carried both my bags to the taxi outside. Madame Morel had loaned me a third bag. With all my new purchases, I needed another suitcase to take everything home.

"I promise I'll ship the bag back to you once I'm home," I volunteered.

"Oh, no. Please keep it for now," Madame Morel insisted. "If we come to the United States someday, we'll need another bag for our return trip."

I thanked Madame Morel for hosting me and also for

taking me shopping. I said I hoped that we might do that again sometime.

"Certainly Charlotte," she said graciously. "… My dear American daughter." I felt a huge lump in my throat as I threw my arms around her and gave her a big hug. It had been so special going shopping with Sophie's mom. (I love my dad but he is not a great shopper of girls' clothes— they seem to befuddle him.) Madame Morel bent down and kissed me on the cheek. "Charlotte, you will always have a home in Paris." It was the most meaningful thing she could have said. I hugged her one more time.

Monsieur Morel, Sophie, and I got into the cab and set off for the airport. It seemed like no time at all had passed since we had been heading in the opposite direction when I first landed last Sunday. Once we arrived at l'Aéroport Charles de Gaulle, Monsieur made sure I knew where I was going. The check-in desk was just inside the door, and Mr. Morel explained that I was traveling alone and would need an attendant to escort me to my gate.

The taxi beeped, so we had to say good-bye quickly.

Sophie hugged me.

"I'll see you soon, Sophie," I promised, squeezing her tightly. Suddenly, the lump in my throat was back.

"*Bon voyage, mon amie,*" Sophie choked, hugging me one last time.

I waved at the taxi pulling away from the curb and then headed inside the airport to begin my journey home.

★

Exhausted from the events of the week, I slept through almost the entire flight back to Boston.

As we were getting ready to land at Logan Airport, I woke up, feeling like I had imagined the whole trip. But then the flight attendant pulled my new coat from the overhead bin, and it all became real to me again.

Dad was waiting for me outside the security area after I collected my baggage and passed through Customs. I jumped into his arms, hugging him tightly.

"Charlotte, I missed you so much," he said into my hair. "Were you this tall when you left? I swear you've grown two inches and … you look … a bit different," he declared, holding me at arm's length. "Did you get your hair cut or something?"

I smiled. "No, Dad. Check out my new coat and shoes. Thanks to Madame Morel … she insisted on taking me shopping."

"Well, Madame Morel is a very generous woman with a big heart. You look very grown up—very fancy too!"

I smiled.

"Wait a minute, you ARE very grown up. I don't think I like this one bit. What happened to the cute little five-year-old girl who hid behind me and refused to look at other people?" Dad asked, throwing his arm around my shoulder as we headed out the door.

"Dad!"

"Well … what can I say? I'd like you to stay my little girl. For a few more years at least."

❧

I leaned my head against his shoulder as we continued to walk. I wondered if he was right. Maybe I had grown up a bit. I hoped at least that my klutzy days were finally behind me.

"I'm sorry you didn't find Orangina," Dad said as we headed toward the car.

"But we did *see* Orangina," I told him as we got into the car.

"You did?"

"Yes … on the very last day. We started and ended each day of searching the same way … at our houseboat."

"How is the houseboat?"

"It looks the same … except there aren't any geraniums in the kitchen window and the back deck has so many bikes piled up that there isn't any room for the wicker chair."

"Ah … Paris."

"Yup … the Seine still has that same old magic, Dad. The more I thought about it, the more I realized that Orangina really belongs to the Seine. He loves that river so much."

"Don't we all. So you saw him by the river?"

"ON the river."

"On the river?"

"Yes. He was sitting like a hood ornament on the front of a barge. You know, one of those farmer's barges. He probably latched on to the farmer and the barge just as he did to us and our houseboat."

"Did the farmer look like a nice fellow?"

"Actually … he looks even grumpier than Yuri. Sophie calls him *mauvais Caractère*—Sourpuss. He does look like a sourpuss. But I think he's got a good heart. Orangina looked well cared for. At least we know he's being fed and has a roof over his head to stay out of the rain, which he hates so much."

Dad laughed. It was quiet for awhile as we drove by the Charles River toward our house in Brookline.

"You know what? I always blamed those boys for chasing Orangina away, but maybe he actually ran away on his own … because he wanted to stay close to the Seine," I told Dad as we pulled up in front of our house. I gazed up at the yellow Victorian with its blue shutters.

"It's good to be home," I said as I got out of the car. "But I'm not so sure Orangina would feel at home here."

"Perhaps you're right. Maybe it's just as well," Dad said as we walked to the door.

"Why do you say that?"

"Well, someone here missed you an awful lot."

Dad opened the door and Marty began dancing around my heels, wiggling with joy. I tried to avoid stepping on him, which was hard because every time I put my foot down it seemed that Marty was right underneath it. Dodging Marty and juggling my bags, I tripped on the edge of the Oriental rug in the foyer and tumbled to the floor. So much for Paris making me less klutzy. Marty jumped up on my stomach and licked my face. *Home sweet home*, I thought as I gave my little pooch a very big hug.

Charlotte in *Paris* Book Extras

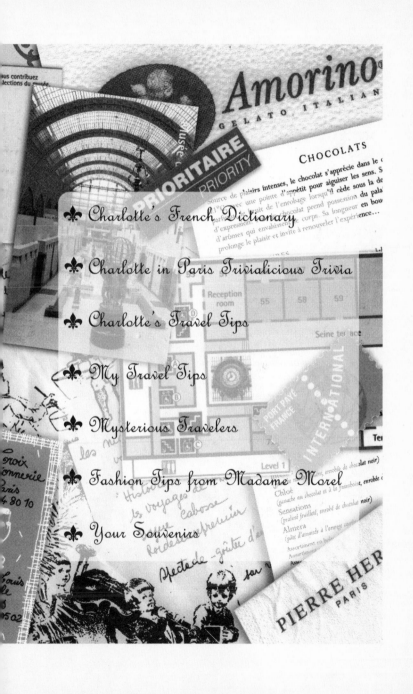

Charlotte Ramsey

Charlotte's French Dictionary - Everything You Need To Get Around Paris ... Sort Of!

Bonjour mes amies!

I had the most amazing time in Paris ...
the memories will stay with me always.
When you travel, it's always a good
idea to brush up on the native language.
Here are some French words and phrases
I used during my Parisian adventure ...
I hope you have fun learning the language
of love!

bisous,
Charlotte

A

À bientôt: (p. 177)—see you soon.

A la prochaine fois: (p. 183)—until next time.

Allons-y!: (p. 164)—let's go!

Amuse gueule: (p. 62) noun—appetizer.

Au revoir: (p. 6, 50, 101, 171, 177) exclamation—Goodbye.

B

Baguette: (p. 62, 71, 115) noun—French loaf of bread.

Bien sûr!: (p. 59)—of course!

Bienvenue à bord: (p. 31)—Welcome aboard.

Bienvenue à Paris: (p. 66)—Welcome to Paris.

Bisous: (p. 2, 67, 103) noun—kisses

Bon appétit: (p. 63)—Enjoy your meal.

Bonjour: (p. 4, 55, 71, 83, 106, 130) exclamation—Hello.

Bonjour ma chérie!: (p. 32)—Hello my dear!

Bonjour mes amies!: (p. 102)—Hello my friends!

Bonne chance aujourd'hui: (p. 123)—good luck today.

Bonne nuit: (p. 102, 180)—Good night.

Bonsoir: (p. 28) exclamation—Good evening.

Bon voyage: (p. 17, 20, 22, 28, 175)—Have a good trip.

Bon voyage, mon amie: (p. 184)—Have a good trip, my friend.

Boule de fourrure orange: (p. 54)—orange fur-ball.

Bourguignon: (p. 63, 98) adjective—from Burgundy; a dish including mushrooms and parsley.

Brie: (p. 99)—a soft French cheese.

✤

C

Cacahouètes: (p. 85) noun—peanuts.

Cantal: (p. 99)—hard yellow French cheese (like Cheddar).

Ça va?: (p. 83)—How are you?

Célèbre: (p. 130) adjective—famous.

Ce n'est pas nécessaire: (p. 107)—It's not necessary.

Ce n'est pas vrai: (p. 140)—It can't be true.

C'est bien: (p. 170)—That's good.

C'est bizarre: (p. 136)—That's odd.

C'est délicieux: (p. 91)—It's delicious.

C'est quoi: (p. 136)—What is that …

C'est une tragédie!: (p. 147)—It is a tragedy!

C'est vrai?: (p. 139)—Is it true?

Chic: (p. 40, 56, 79) adjective—fashionable.

Chuchoteurs: (p. 85, 102, 179) noun—whisperers.

Comme un rêve: (p. 31)—just like a dream.

Crème brûlé: (p. 64)—burned cream (dessert).

Croque-monsieurs: (p. 115)—grilled ham and cheese sandwich.

D

Dans tes rêves: (p. 179)—in your dreams.

Démodé: (p. 74) adjective—out of fashion.

Deux euros pour trois, deux euros pour trois:
(p. 155)—two euros for three, two euros for three.

Doux de Montagne: (p. 63)—Sweet Mountain (cheese).

Du coeur: (p. 169)—of the heart.

E

En français: (p. 55)—in French.

Entrez: (p. 125) verb—Enter; Come in.

Épicerie: (p. 62, 120, 121) noun—grocery.

Escargots: (p. 60) noun—snails.

Escargots à la bourguignonne (p. 98)—Burgundian snails; snails with mushrooms and parsley.

Excusez moi: (p. 91, 147)—Excuse me.

F

Face à face: (p. 165)—face to face.

Fantastique: (p. 69) adjective—terrific.

Formidable: (p. 33, 173) adjective—awesome.

Fromage: (p. 122) noun—cheese.

G

Génial: (p. 108, 130) adjective—awesome.

Gros, gros bisous: (p. 103)—big, big kisses.

I

Incroyable: (p. 121) adjective—incredible.

J

Je ne comprends pas: (p. 139)—I don't understand.

Je ne sais pas: (p. 121)—I don't know.

Je ne sais quoi: (p. 39)—I don't know what; something.

Je sais: (p. 152)—I know.

Je suis arrivée à Paris!: (p. 67)—I arrived in Paris!

✣

Je t'en prie: (p. 50, 65)—you're welcome.

Jour pluvieux: (p. 120)—rainy day.

L

La bise: (p. 32, 50, 55, 97) noun—the kiss.

La découverte: (p. 133) noun—the discovery.

La gendarmerie: (p. 143, 163) noun—the police.

La meilleure nouvelle: (p. 1)—the best news ever.

La minuterie (les minuteries): (p. 172, 173, 174) noun— the time switch, the time switches.

La petite: (p. 156) adjective—little one (feminine).

La rentrée: (p. 82)—back to school.

La soirée: (p. 172) noun—the party.

La soupe aux oignions: (p. 99)—onion soup.

Le dernier cri: (p. 70)—the latest fashion.

Le petit-déjeuner est prêt: (p. 57)—Breakfast is ready.

Le petit navir: (p. 97)—little boat.

Les bouquinistes: (p. 108) noun—secondhand booksellers.

Les moules au diable: (p. 99)—mussels in a spicy sauce.

Les rues de Paris: (p. 62)—the streets of Paris.

Les temps s'écoule comme de l'eau: (p. 88)—Time is like a river.

M

Ma chérie: (p. 32, 50, 71, 77)—my dear.

Ma copine: (p. 37)—my friend.

Mademoiselle: (p. 28, 155, 170) title—Miss.

Magnifique: (p. 79, 101) adjective—magnificent.

Mais alors: (p. 56)—but then.

Mais oui: (p. 39, 53)—yes, of course.

Maman: (p. 2, 62, 92, 97, 118, 176) noun—mom.

Marché aux puces: (p. 40) noun—flea market.

Mauvais Caractère: (p. 156, 160, 187)—sourpuss.

Mauvaise couleur: (p. 77)—bad color.

Merci: (p. 28, 56, 64, 131, 177) exclamation—Thank you.

Merci beaucoup: (p. 65, 87, 130)—Thank you very much.

Mes amis: (p. 87)—my friends.

Mesdemoiselles: (p. 169) title—Miss (plural).

Métro: (p. 37, 73, 74, 80, 156) noun—subway.

Moi aussi: (p. 59)—me too.

Mon amie: (p. 54, 115, 130, 140, 159, 184)—my friend.

Monsieur: (p. 130, 131) title—Mr.

N

N'est-ce pas?: (p. 72, 80, 140, 174)—don't you think?

Non: (p. 112, 114, 136) interrogative, adverb—isn't it (she, he)?; no.

Nous sommes arrivés: (p. 54)—Here we are.

O

Omelette au fromage: (p. 71)—omelette with cheese.

Oui: (p. 6, 64, 127, 142, 147) adverb—yes.

Ouistiti: (p. 122) noun—marmoset; a small monkey from South America.

�֍

P

Papier-mâché: (p. 129)—paper mâché

Pardonez moi: (p. 154)—Pardon me.

Parfait: (p. 79) adjective—perfect.

Parfum: (p. 32) noun—perfume.

Pas à pas: (p. 106)—step by step.

Pas une minute à perdre: (p. 150)—The clock is ticking (not a moment to lose).

Perdu et trouvé: (p. 146)—lost and found.

Q

Qualité: (p. 77) noun—quality.

Quelle horreur!: (p. 77)—How horrible!

Quelle imagination!: (p. 140)—What imagination!

Qu'est-ce que j'ai vu?: (p. 110)—What did I see?

R

Regardez!: (p. 110)—Look!

Regardez Mesdames, mademoiselles, messieurs!: (p. 155)—Look ladies, young ladies, gentlemen!

Regarde! Regarde!: (p. 160)—Look! Look!

Riche: (p. 130) adjective—rich.

Rien: (p. 54) noun—nothing.

Russe: (p. 99) adjective—Russian; dessert made with Bavarian cream and ladyfingers.

S

Splendide: (p. 77) adjective—magnificent.

Stupides bateaux: (p. 89)—stupid boats.

Souvenir: (p. 112, 129, 158, 171) noun—souvenir.

T

Tome de Savoie: (p. 99)—strong-flavored yellow French cheese.

Très américain, n'est-pas?: (p. 101)—very American, isn't it?

Très belles: (p. 98)—very beautiful.

Très bizarre!: (p. 66)—very weird!

Très chic: (p. 79)—very fashionable.

Très chouette: (p. 101)—really great.

Très fatiguée: (p. 55)—very tired.

Très français: (p. 79)—very French.

Très serieuse: (p. 149)—very serious.

Trop lourd: (p. 77)—too heavy.

Tu dois manger: (p. 154)—you must eat.

U

Un chapeau: (p. 78) noun—a hat.

Un petit cadeau: (p. 75)—a little gift.

Une dernière chance: (p. 153)—one last chance.

Une très grande ville: (p. 156)—a huge city.

✤

V

Viens: (p. 131) verb—Come (informal).

Vive la différence: (p. 53)—Here's to our differences.

Voilà: (p. 55, 121) exclamation—There you go!

Voyage incroyable: (p. 35)—fabulous voyage.

Can You Count in French?

1. Un
2. Deux
3. Trois
4. Quatre
5. Cinq
6. Six
7. Sept
8. Huit
9. Neuf
10. Dix
11. Onze
12. Douze
13. Treize
14. Quatorze
15. Quinze
16. Seize
17. Dix-sept
18. Dix-huit
19. Dix-neuf
20. Vinqt

Charlotte in Paris trivialicious trivia

1. **Paris is the City of ...**
A. Fashion
B. Light
C. Croissants
D. Cheese

2. **What actress did Cary Grant's character fall in love with in the movie "Charade?"**
A. Audrey Hepburn
B. Sophia Loren
C. Katherine Hepburn
D. Isabella Rossellini

3. **What did Maeve give Charlotte as a going away present?**
A. Swedish Fish
B. A French movie poster
C. A pen on a cord
D. Several tiny plastic ducks

4. **What was the name of the Englishman Charlotte met on the plane to Paris?**
A. Mr. Peckham
B. Mr. Smith
C. Mr. Wilshire
D. None of the above

5. **What did Madame Morel serve for dinner on Charlotte's first night in Paris?**
A. Beef bourguignon
B. A cheese course
C. Crême brûlé
D. All of the above

6. **Who are the Parisian Whisperers (like Anna and Joline)?**
A. Céleste and Chantal
B. Dominique and Fifi
C. Gigi and Simone
D. Sandrine and Brigitte

7. **What image do Parisians think of to make them smile for photographs?**
A. Monkeys
B. Cheese
C. Poodles
D. Escargots

8. **What does the street vendor they call "Sourpuss" sell?**
A. Fruits and vegetables
B. Medical supplies
C. Fish
D. Old books

9. **What does Charlotte find inside her Picasso coloring book?**
A. A picture of Nick
B. A sketch
C. A poem
D. A treasure map

10. **Where does Charlotte last see Orangina?**
A. At the Eiffel Tower
B. At the cinema
C. In a woman's shopping bag
D. On a barge

11. **Which of the following foods are not originally French?**
A. French fries
B. French onion soup
C. French toast
D. Beef bourguignon

12. **We know Orangina is Charlotte's cat. What kind of food is Orangina?**
A. Chicken
B. Pizza
C. Carrot
D. Soft drink

11. A. French fries 12. D. Soft drink
7. A. Monkeys 8. A. Fruits and Vegetables 9. B. A sketch 10. D. On a barge
4. A Mr. Peckham 5. D. All of the above 6. A. Céleste and Chantal
ANSWERS: 1. B. Light **2. A.** Audrey Hepburn **3. C.** A pen on a cord

Charlotte's Travel Tips

1. Make a list of the things you need to bring.

2. Check them off as you pack.

3. Pack light, only what you can easily carry.

4. Take something to do on the plane. A book, or, if you get air or car sick, a game or coloring book.

5. Drink a lot of water.

6. Wear comfortable clothes.

My Personal Travel Tips

❧

My Travel Speak

Interesting phrases I have learned during my own travels ...

Phrases I would teach travelers coming to my town …

✦

Fashion Tips From Madame Morel

1. SHOES: Pick shoes that won't be *démode* (out of fashion) by next year. Choose the shoe that makes you feel confident and comfortable

2. COATS: Quality counts. Know what colors bring out your complexion and the color of your eyes.

My Special Fashion Advice To The World ...

Draw or paste Your Favorite Look

Souvenirs

njour

Add your souvenirs ...

♥ ooh la la! *Paris*

stationery.

www.beaconstreetgirls.com

"bon voyage" purple velvet overnight bag with matching backpack.

Messenger bag.

...llow with book &
...ght & Paris clutch.

You'll just love what I found in Paris!

Meet the Beacon Street Girls ... they're real, they're fun
—they're just like you! ❀

www.beaconstreetgirls.com

Who's Who

BSG

Katani Summers
a.k.a. Kgirl ... Katani
has a strong fashion
sense and business
savvy. She is stylish,
loyal & cool.

Avery Madden
Avery is passionate
about all sports and
animal rights. She
is energetic, optimistic
& outspoken.

Charlotte Ramsey
A self-acknowledged
"klutz" and an aspiring
writer, Charlotte is all
too familiar with being
the new kid in town.
She is intelligent,
worldly & curious.

Isabel Martinez
Her ambition is to be
an artist. She was the
last to join the Beacon
Street Girls. She is
artistic, sensitive &
kind.

Maeve Kaplan-Taylor
Maeve wants to be
a movie star. Bubbly
and upbeat, she
wears her heart on her
sleeve. She is enter-
taining, friendly & fun.

Ms. Razzberry Pink
The stylishly pink
proprietor of the "Think
Pink" boutique is chic,
gracious & charming.

Marty
The adopted best
dog friend of the
Beacon Street Girls is
feisty, cuddly & suave.

Happy Lucky Thingy and
alter ego Mad Nasty Thingy
Marty's favorite chew
toy is known to reveal
its alter ego when
shaken too roughly.
He is most often
happy.

more on beaconstreetgirls.com

Check out all the BSG books!

Book 1 - Worst Enemies/Best Friends

Yikes! As if being the new girl isn't bad enough ...
Charlotte just made the biggest cafeteria blunder in the
history of Abigail Adams Junior High. Will Charlotte,
Katani, Avery, and Maeve become best friends? Or worst
enemies?

Book 2 - Bad News/Good News

Charlotte can't believe it. Her father wants to move away
again, and the timing couldn't be worse for the Beacon
Street Girls. Does this add up to good news? Or bad
news? Find out in the Beacon Street Girls' latest adventure.

Book 3 - Letters from the Heart

Life seems perfect for Maeve and Avery ... until they find
out that in seventh grade, the world can turn upside
down just like that. Will divorce, boy trouble, dog trouble,
and the Queens of Mean ruin everything, or will letters
from the heart pull them through their latest adventure?

Book 4 - Out of Bounds

Can the Beacon Street Girls bring the house down at
Abigail Adams Junior High's Talent Show? Or will the
Queens of Mean steal the show? The Beacon Street Girls
face their toughest challenges yet and show everyone
that sometimes you have to take things out of bounds to
make things right again.

Book 5 - Promises, Promises

Elections for class president are underway, and the
Beacon Street Girls are right in the middle of it all. The
drama escalates when election posters start to disappear. Will the candidate with the best ideas win the election, or will it come down to something else?

Book 6 - Lake Rescue
Big time fun awaits the Beacon Street Girls and the rest of the seventh grade. The class is heading to Lake Rescue in New Hampshire for outdoor education. Will Nick's attention to Isabel make Charlotte wonder about her own feelings? Will the physical challenges of this outdoor adventure prove too much for one seventh-grade girl?

Book 7 - Freaked Out
The party of the year is just around the corner, and the Beacon Street Girls are in the middle of the excitement. What happens when the party invitations are given out ... but not to everyone? Will the party of the year get way out of hand?

Book 8 - Lucky Charm
Marty is missing! The BSG begin a desperate search for their beloved doggie mascot which leads them to an unexpected and famous person. At the same time, Katani and Kelley's new riding stable is in danger of closing. Will the BSG be able to help? Or will their solution create a difficult friendship dilemma.

Book 9 - Fashion Frenzy
Katani and Maeve head to New York City to experience a teen fashion show. Meanwhile, back in Boston, the seventh-grade class heads to the Museum of Fine Arts to explore the Egyptian mummies. Katani and Maeve learn the hard way that fashion is all about self-expression and being true to one's self.

Have you seen

www.beaconstreetgirls.com ?

BEACON STREET GIRLS

MEET THE BSG   EXPLORE THEIR WORLD   PLAY GAMES   DOWNLOAD STUFF   BOOKS

B.F.F.

new!
Make a friendship bracelet

BSG   Welcom

BSG Poll

Who do you feel mos like today?

○ Maeve

○ Av

○ Katani

○ Isa

○ Charlotte

Take our poll and see what other BSG girls said.

done

August 28, 2006   **Top Picks**

SECRET TOWER
Find out more about the secret BSG meeting spot!

ISABEL'S RECIPES
You don't want to miss these scrumptious treats from Isabel's kitchen!

BSG JIGSAW JAM
We've got more puzzles! Help put the pieces together.

AVERY'S BLOG
This girl speaks her mind ... about dogs, sports, and what rules she'd like to change.

More **FUN!**

Games   Quizzes
Recipes   Shopping
Crafts   Contests

Which BSG are you?

bff te

Pick the phrase that describes you best ...
then go over to **www.beaconstreetgirls.com**
to find out who you are most like.

Organized to a T,
you're the planner
of the group, with
a flair for fashion
and business.

Your artistic and
sometimes a little
shy ... but would do
anything for you're
friends!

You're a total sports nut, always on
the go, and a little outspoken at times.

Dreamy, and
creative, and
sometimes a klutz.
You love writing
in your journal
and looking at
the stars.

A born entertainer,
you love to make
your friends laugh.
A passion for
movies, music,
and boys!

Avery

Isabel

Charlotte

Katani

Maeve

Video
Music
Secret Goodies

BSG

... and all the BSG news

Join the Club!

Only Club BSG Members Get:

❀ FREE Welcome kit & gift
exclusive contests & sweepstakes ❀
❀ sneak peeks at upcoming books & products
vote on your favorite things ❀
❀ access to "secret" pages
special birthday surprises ❀
... and more!

Join Now! totally FREE!

www.beaconstreetgirls.com

Don't forget to visit
www.beaconstreetgirls.com
We have games, quizzes,
and a BSG shop!